The
Louisville
Review

Volume 88
Fall 2020

The Louisville Review

Editor	Sena Jeter Naslund
Associate Editor	Flora K. Schildknecht
Managing Editor	Amy Foos Kapoor
Guest Poetry Editor	Jonathan Weinert
Guest Fiction Editor	Robert Sachs
Cornerstone Editor	Betsy Woods
Intern	Jared M. Foos

The newly independent TLR publishes two volumes each year: spring and fall. Visit our website for complete guidelines, back issues, subscriptions, and more: www.louisvillereview.org.

Like us on Facebook for up to date information about each issue, news on contributors, and more: www.facebook.com/TheLouisvilleReview.

Follow us on Twitter @TheLouRev.

Questions? Please note our new mailing and email addresses:

The Louisville Review Corporation
1436 St. James Court #1
Louisville, KY 40208
managingeditor@louisvillereview.org

This issue: $10 ppd
Sample copy: $5 ppd
Subscriptions: One year, $18; two years, $36
Foreign subscribers, please add $30/year for shipping.

The text and the cover printed in the United States. Cover design by Jonathan Weinert. Cover photo: "Jaisalmer Fort Overlooking City" by Rajat Kapoor.

I must begin this note with a HUGE Thank You to poet Ellyn Lichvar, who served so ably and so long as Managing Editor for *The Louisville Review*, under the sponsorship of Spalding University.

In the next breath, I thank Amy Foos Kapoor, who also holds the MFA from Spalding, as our new Managing Editor, as we embrace our new status as an independent literary magazine, as well as Associate Editor Flora K. Schildknecht, for her many-faceted support and assistance in establishing our new status.

Founded in 1976, by myself and two undergraduate students, Bonnie Cherry and Tom Willett, at the University of Louisville, *The Louisville Review* continues to welcome unsolicited submissions in poetry and fiction. Every issue includes work by highly published writers alongside those publishing for the first time, from throughout the United States and abroad. Submissions are made electronically twice a year. Please see our website for more information. We continue to publish work by students in grades K-12 in the Cornerstone section of the magazine.

When I gave a talk recently at the University of Kentucky (just before the Covid-19 pandemic), a faculty member poet whom I didn't know came up to thank me for publishing her first poem. I was rather surprised and rummaged around in memory for a clue. Then she added, "It was many years ago in the Writing for Children section; it gave me the encouragement I needed to continue writing poetry." Such revelations, seemingly out of the blue, certainly encourage me to carry on the editorial work that I have enjoyed so much, over the decades, as I continue with my own fiction writing.

Unique to this issue, #88 of *The Louisville Review*, is a short essay by poet and guest poetry editor Jonathan Weinert, which he wrote at my request. Jonathan also served as poetry editor for our issue #85; when I read those poems, something strange began to happen. I began to feel that the poems, not the poets, were somehow speaking to each other. I've read that in a vast forest some trees communicate, underground, over distance, through their astonishing intertwined network of roots. They send information, and alerts. In the poems that Jonathan had selected, it seemed to me the words themselves, unknown to the poets, had things to say to each other—to augment, or explore related feelings/thoughts in a different manner. When I asked Jonathan about such a strange subterranean connection, after publication, he concurred.

And then we decided he would select the poems for this issue, #88, and if a similar phenomenon presented itself, he would write an essay about it. Is there a collective, contemporary consciousness? Do our words know themselves and each other? Please don't miss reading Jonathan Weinert's brief but amazing essay, focusing on language use and imagery, after reading the poetry section.

Having been selected by two different editors, the fiction in this issue spans a wide range of tone, subject matter, length. Readers may need to be something of an acrobat to swing through a variety of fiction-reader-stances in order to enjoy the circus. To enter the world of fiction, readers are accustomed to assuming a "willing suspension of disbelief" and to enter the world created by fiction as real, and as really mattering. But perhaps fiction and non-fiction are good enough bedfellows that they can wear each other's clothes, even pass for one another. Readers will find that the final story here reverses the arrow—presenting first as bold-faced history, but then. . . . Are fact and fiction mirror images of one another? What about the ontological status of all that purports to be history?

I'd like to thank the guest editors, who, along with myself in fiction, selected the poetry and fiction for *TLR* #88:

ROBERT SACHS' fiction has appeared in *The Louisville Review*, the *Chicago Quarterly Review*, the *Free State Review*, the *Great Ape Journal*, and the *Delmarva Review*. He holds an MFA in Writing from Spalding University. His story, "Vondelpark," was nominated for a Pushcart Prize in 2017. His story, "Yo-Yo Man," was a Fiction Finalist in the 2019 Tiferet Writing Contest. Read more at www.roberthsachs.com.

JONATHAN WEINERT is the author of *A Slow Green Sleep* (forthcoming 2021), winner of the Saturnalia Books Editors Prize, *In the Mode of Disappearance* (2008), winner of the Nightboat Poetry Prize, and *Thirteen Small Apostrophes*, a chapbook. He is co-editor, with Kevin Prufer, of *Until Everything Is Continuous Again: American Poets on the Recent Work of W.S. Merwin*. A graduate of Brandeis University and the Spalding MFA in Writing program, Jonathan lives and works in Stow, Massachusetts.

BETSY WOODS is the author of the upcoming novel, *Strong Moon Tonight*. Her work has appeared in literary journals internationally. She is the writer-in-residence at the Waldorf School of New Orleans.

–Sena Jeter Naslund, Editor

Table of Contents

Poetry

Guest Poetry Editor's Note

FICTION

BOOK REVIEW

CORNERSTONE
work by writers K-12

Peter Grandbois

I AM DONE BEING THIS TINY HOUSE

Except this body that opens

                                to desire

Except this window that opens

                                to rain.

Simon Perchik

*

All wood floats though this shack
hems you in—it's hopeless
drinking water at every meal

pointing to beaches, channels, boats
till slowly they row end to end
as shadows, half alongside, half

something to hold that is not sunlight
thrown far off to build a crater
from these empty chairs—you thrive

on rage :a well that gave all its thirst
to the scent near the open window
named after the walls and ceiling.

Laurie Welch

Sonnet for the Murderous Plains

This place is a big black closet,
an infinity of hat boxes
Mab stashed inside.
Look, she's waving

a white flag for fake or a wonder so big
we can't take it seriously.
She's flummoxed just trying to
distinguish her own phases.

What is it again that we care about here?
The flowers? Really?
But she pickets. She riots in a collage of glitches
that don't exist, that don't exit.

Sometimes something breaks loose,
a goof maybe. And we learn how to share it.

Tom Hunley

Fifty

All morning I gather the parts of me.
A wedding ring lodges beneath a swollen knuckle.
At least I'm not in one of those old bodies
that chases young bodies, a bird that doesn't recognize
the window between himself and that sweet parakeet.
On the other hand my other hand writes
and remembers how to grip a tennis racquet.
My feet search for socks to cram themselves into
like songs into three radio-friendly minutes.
My mouth is an open door, my throat a foyer,
my belly a rec room. Bring more chairs, more chairs.
Earlier, my ear tried to alert me
to a new way to disappear but it was fooling itself—
I'm a noise that's not going anywhere.
At least my eyes have stayed in my head,
which, at least, has held onto some hair.
Once a year I give blood like a Christmas present
I hope to get back. Aches ride up and down
the elevator of my body, unsure what floor
to settle on. There's a pill for this. Side effects
may include loss of speed and parents.
My students ogle their phones when they could watch
theater-style as I come apart like a cloud of smoke,
and who could blame them? More interesting to read
Lady Gaga's tweets or play Diamond Mine.
I tell them to savor each breath the way
an alcoholic savors the last shot in the bottle.
Class, one minute you're playing egg toss;
the next minute you're the egg.

Simon Perchik

*

You leave a fist, its knock
elsewhere and no one to let you in
the way her name on the door

has grown huge, fed hillsides
and the grass too is covered
with granite :her small room

filled with season after season
and each finger curled
held back, asking how cold is it

–it's everywhere though your arms
still open out and all these doors
at once, let you stand in front

listening to a procession—one pit
filled with its echo and mourners
empty handed, hungry, cramped.

Katerina Stoykova

THE UNUSED PORTION

of your fatherhood lays
like new shoes in the attic.
Looks uncomfortable.

Marci Rae Johnson

Praying Naked

There's so little light to help us see,
just the blue of this small screen barely reaching

beyond my fingertips to the edge of longing.

The cold, plastic case is unpliable,
unlike your flesh   in my mind

warm beneath my hands,
your quick pulse   the sound of your voice

when you're saying *more* &   *whole.*

This night of the soul is just dark enough
that our minds forget themselves   dismiss

the stumbling, graceless day where no words
were the right ones to say   every breath

impossible to take as deeply as the body needs.

Here you can stand outside yourself,
remember nothing   think

nothing   body light, ecstatic rising up
to this one vision of heaven.

The only one we're bound to see.

Maxima Kahn

MEDITATIONS ON DESIRE

your body is my paper
i want its white music all over my mind
i watch how my desire erases me
how i consume myself with longing

i want its white music all over my mind
and to think i have invented you
how i consume myself with longing
your body obstructs me

even as i think i have invented you
i cannot equal you with any aspect of mind
your body my obstruction
like a *koan* you frustrate my every attempt

mind alone cannot equal you
you wound me with the music i invest your body with
like a koan you frustrate my attempts
why is everyone so calm?

wound me with the music i invest your body with
in my dreams i invent and re-invent you
how can everyone stay so calm?
i will use you as my mirror

in my dreams i invent and re-invent you
i will make of you the poem i need to write
you my mirror
wanting you to want me and imagining that you don't

i will make of you the poem i need to write
i enact my own undoing
in wanting you to want me and imagining that you don't
but equally so when i imagine that you do

i enact my own undoing
i want you to obliterate my mind
but equally so when i imagine that you do
i cannot enter you

obliterate my mind
shall we talk about the body, the site of all desiring?
i cannot enter you
the blood's insistent fire, cells' clamor, skin's howl

this body, site of all desiring
i've heard your delicate, inconsistent music
the blood's insistent fire, cells' clamor, skin's howl
carmen perpetuum, continuous song

i've heard the delicate, inconsistent music
of desire that unmakes and remakes us
carmen perpetuum, continuous song
i think it is the search for the missing parts of ourselves

desire that remakes and unmakes us
that we project on the screens of other bodies and on the page
this search for the missing parts of ourselves
trying to re-create the lost unity

that we project on the screens of other bodies and on the page
trying to ascend to a world of perfection
trying to re-create the lost unity
however momentary

trying to ascend to a world of perfection
what is the line, after all? elegant, beguiling shape
however momentary
how it makes me alternately all-powerful then unworthy

what is the line's elegant, beguiling shape?
how it makes me doubt myself
alternately all-powerful then unworthy
in one moment full of omnipotent joy, in the next a blank space

how it makes me doubt myself
and you, the perfect lover, who will satisfy all desire
in one moment full of omnipotent joy, in the next a blank space
but *why you?* that question troubles me

you, the perfect lover, who will satisfy all desire
i want you to get in my way, deep in
but why you? that question troubles me
i'm looking for the perfect word

get in my way, deep in
there is no winning in the game of desire
i'm looking for the perfect word
or what is it we would win?

there is no winning in the game of desire
we will have to give up the project of redemption
or what is it we would win?
there is no hope for poetry

we will have to give up the project of redemption
i watch how my desire erases me
there is no hope for poetry
your body is my paper.

Amy L. Fair

REQUIESCAT

He raised the hair
on my pale arms,
then raised my dress.

He put his mouth down
 on me, pinned me flat—
sometimes with barely more
than the weight of prayer.

My sparrow's heart
could do nothing,
my sisters;
he could have pulled
a grave up over my body
like a quilt.

Amy L. Fair

Scorpions and Grasshoppers

She fell in a faint,
silent but for the light thump
of her slight weight
on the floor.
I thought about the sound
of gas burners
catching flame,
and it was like that—
low and dangerous.

She said in those seconds
of darkness, she could see.
Landing near a brilliant scorpion,
she dreamed of grasshoppers
and weddings,
and of marrying the ghost
of a man she once knew.

David Romanda

MILLION REASONS

She tells me
she has
a million reasons to leave.
A million, I say.
OK, she says,
I've got six reasons.

David Romanda

Around Town

I've been having these dreams, she says.
I'm cycling naked around town and nobody
seems to notice or care that I'm naked.
Then she says, I don't know. Maybe I wasn't
loved enough as a child.

Peter Grandbois

Sometimes late at night

When trees speak in shadows,
I ask—

Is that me crawling out
of the hoot owl's moan?

Or falling like fish
upon the river
in the dead of winter?

Why do I wrap myself
in ruins?

And why does silence
curl itself into
fists that beat down
all that remains?

I want to understand
the geometry of stone
that rings my sleep,

to sound the choir
of crickets,
envoys from the dark muck
of memory, or
the land of the dead—

both parts of the same distant
song.

Anna Idelevich

Was quiet on the moonlit path

Was quiet on the moonlit path
and poured lingonberry juice into the water
half-wild beast,
half-killed century,
snow and scarlet fur,
for you, for you.

Burned as much as he could
and by morning, broken by a star, lay down
on the cuts of the paws,
cradle of sleep . . .
My paper night
and love winter.

John A. Nieves

BOLE (ITERATION 8)

The reason for the footprints   that appeared
in the forest, we were   told, was that the roots
of the trees got lonely and sucked   down the soil
to show us where to stand, how   to visit. The neighbor
swore the branches   waved along the fresh-pressed
path like pale   green emergency lighting. The whole
woods had gone will   o' the wisp, the holes
in the trunks all   a-whisper. And I would get in
so much trouble   for not being
afraid, for hopping in   the slots that could have
fit two of my feet. There   was a small fox I could
sometimes find down   by the brook. Once, I even
saw it drink. I know   now those tracks had to be
made by someone, that the fox could   have been
the far lesser danger, but even   with that I find
the urge to cheer for the younger   me for wandering
deep into where I may not have come   back. And I admit
I have imagined those   footfalls in the black earth
were made by now me, some future   charity
to lead me   then to this.

Jason Tandon

LOONS

Why is it such a pleasure
when they dive
to scan the surface for where
they might
           re-appear

and be wrong
every time?

Angie Macri

Woodland Margin

The girl who disappeared in redbuds common on the mountain
found sky on the ground, not a lake,
but the heavens themselves, fallen.
The bales in the valley burned
in frost where last summer they had broken
bottles with bottles
for fun. As if stones spoke, air not as warm as their surface
froze for a moment when hit with sunlight, much like her breath
as she entered the redbuds.
Below and long before her, stone leftover
from the church had been made into root cellars.
The widow sat by the empty chair.

Laine Derr

JAWBONE GRASS

Wait, hold on.
Not fittin' to run,
they came in smooth,
flesh with a tether on.

I've been pulling weeds,
outlining the dead
who have a gift of tongues.

Jawbone grass chanting as children
marked in lively rhyme: Red Rover,
Red Rover, our hands are clover.

Margarita Cruz

Hospital Window

Orange lifts itself from the forest, unsticks
shadow feet pulling trees and deer up
into the sky it becomes bright, clear. No stars
left except the big one as we turn towards it.
I wake up to the dead again here.
Even the foxes hide from my window.
Everything silent except for the AC
a medical cart in the hallway wooshes.
I am laying on my belly for the first time in weeks,
the scab on my heart heals.
Still reminds me that ghosts don't keep scars
monsters do, however.

Taylor Zhang

A SOFTER KIND OF DROWNING

I shower in the morning with my
eyes closed, the water hot enough
to leave red imprints on my skin. I have
dreams now—forever, the same:
starched dresses, pockets flat, three girls
staring from across a field. I am always
awake when they come to me, so
maybe I would call them daydreams if
they were not so terrible. Sunday
will come. Legs float out of the water
and blonde heads melt. In the
crushed red of my seat, I pretend
that waking to cold sweats and seeing
children at traffic lights are a part
of my divined future. Desperation
comes most often as a question, yet
who can resist asking: *is this my life?*

Taylor Zhang

Imitation Crab

I own fourteen shirts, five of which are white t-shirts and another five
of which are black turtlenecks. The other four I won't describe for the
sake of suspense.

During my interview, a man compliments my lettuce sleeves (white
t-shirt #3). I tell him where I bought my t-shirt, and out of deference,
ask him where he bought his own, even though it is very ugly. He does
not respond. I ask again. I clear my throat. I grab my lettuce sleeves.
The radio station on his desk orders me to contact my doctor right
away. I burst into tears.

At home, I order a shirt that is exactly like the man's shirt. I have never
been good with boundaries.

Tyler King

READING FRANK O'HARA TO MY GHOST FRIENDS

a boy comes in from
the rain with blood under
his nails. i've seen him before
you know. once at midnight in a field of
goldenrod & dandelions, braced against a bitter october wind,
     he pointed
a finger at the moon and said see,
I told you the harvest would come
early. this is the moon I was born under & all I ever needed was
     an excuse to return.
so we sat shivering all night waiting
for something to happen &
in the morning he found his mother
on the side of a road
crumpled up like bills on the
coffee table. i went to the funeral
without ever asking her name so
i won't tell you his now.

i think you're right, i don't
deserve to be here. this is heaven after
all. but it's still my party. i'll get saved
if I wanna get saved. nobody who
deserves it ever dies you know?
i've been here long enough to see
how the boys turn into poems.
i hope when the next harvest comes
you don't wake me up. i want to see
everybody i miss. i want to
disappoint a low hanging sun.
i want to be brand new forever.

the last time i saw him was in
a museum of only mirrors & he
never said a word. his face became

like every other face. right at the end
it was like the earth let him go.
darkly, he rose while I slept.
i slept until i understood what i
was hoping to see & then
i kept right on sleeping.

Greg Pape

Rebuilding the Temple: Higashi Honganji, Kyoto

*The monk Shinran (1173–1263) founded the Jodo
Shinshu or Pure Land sect of Buddhism on the belief that
Amida Buddha vowed to save all those who sincerely repeated the
phrase* namu amida butsu *or "Praise to Amida Buddha"*

As she stood before the glass display case
(I was looking through from the other side)
where a great coil of black and gray rope
braided from human hair lay she grimaced
and her hand touched her own hair as if
she could feel it being pulled taut and sliced off
just at the scalp as the hundreds of women had,
standing in line to take their turn,
who gave their hair to the monks to braid
into this rope, so much stronger than the hemp
rope that often broke as they pulled the huge
cedar logs down the mountains in the snow.

    First built in Kyoto in 1604 Higashi Honganji temple
    (the Founder's Hall alone is the largest wooden building
    in Kyoto and one of the largest in the world) burned down
    four times, most recently in 1864. The two main buildings,
    Amida Hall and Founder's Hall, were rebuilt in 1895
    with great effort, devotion, and sacrifice.

I thought of the monks chanting as they worked
braiding the precious hair *namu amida butsu*
and the sawyers chanting *namu amida butsu*
as they first approached the great trees
then as they worked in teams to cut them down,
limb them, load them on hand-hewn sleds,
and haul them down the switch-back trails
along the cliffs and around the rocks in the snow
and icy winter winds *namu amida butsu*

dozens of men in lines hauling the logs
with ropes in their hands made of the hair
of their wives, sisters, daughters, mothers
namu amida butsu

    As we left the temple grounds
    we noticed the words written
    in many languages on the outer walls:
    "Now, Life is living you" *namu amida butsu*

Tyler King

REVELATIONS 2

If I call this gospel,
then maybe all the men
coughing hellfire all up
and down Salem &
Gettysburg will lay down their swords and
throw roses at my feet, and maybe
my phone rings all night and I answer it
just once, and it's
a whole city of machine ghosts
wishing me happy birthday

You say my name and I taste
salt, cold honey,
a rotting garden pushes up
through the gaps in my teeth,
I make too many
promises and fall asleep
still hungry

I lay three cards on the table
and you turn over death,
three times in twice as many
years, I blink once
and the world ends,
just like that, and it was all
so bright
until it wasn't, and
you said something I couldn't hear
on the way up, while I was playing
Abel in the end of innocence, and
I get up from my chalk outline,
and ballroom dance, graceless and

blissful, across the surface of the
river, until the noise drowns out

     everything, including this

Marci Rae Johnson

THE LOUDEST POSSIBLE SOUND

is the one you hear in your mind
at night looking out at the deserted parking lot,
the distant streetlight.

It's dark in your head & it seems
there's no one in the world but you.
The empty apartment, the echo

of your steps on the worn wood floor.
The blue of the computer screen
lighting up your face—perhaps

if you work hard enough you'll forget
all the years of loneliness, more potent
for the fact that you were not alone,

that the person who had promised to love
& to cherish, in the next room worked steadily
upon her deceit.

The sound is what you hear even
in your underwater dreams, as you come
sputtering up, trying to catch your breath.

The sound is the measure of your loneliness.
It is the measure of your fear

that you'll never find yourself again,
the one that has wandered so many years
in the depths, out of reach.

But there is an upper limit
to how loud a sound can be—

& you have found, finally, its end.
From here you will swim up to the surface,
though slowly, & sometimes

it will seem to suck you down again,
though it cannot hold you there.

Milica Mijatović

Strawberries

We ate them in the field by the stream
after old man Jocika passed. Funerals,
something we were good at. Someone
made a joke about Jocika's mangled hands,
the way he would pretend to eat his fingers,
master of the noses & thumbs game.
He used to make us laugh. He used to tell us
stories about how he lost his fingers, each
finger a different story, and each story
different every time. The ring on his ring finger
choked his finger to death; he woke one morning
to a missing thumb, searched for days, found
it in his backyard, riddled with ants; he won
first place in a pinky finger beauty contest,
was asked to sit still for a mold, couldn't wait
long, so he cut his pinky off, donated it,
and now it sits in all its glory in a museum
in Helsinki. His contribution to western society.
We grew up when we realized what actually
happened to his hands, and some time after,
his heart burst, the same way strawberries do
when you bite into them just right.

Milica Mijatović

Human Head, Dream

A land mine found him,
and he came back to his fiancé
as a bodiless soldier, only
his head left functioning.
The two of them married
in my backyard, grenade pins
for rings, except he had no
fingers because he had no hands
or arms or shoulders or legs.
And when it came to the kiss,
I picked up his swollen head
and held it to his new wife's lips.

Amy L. Fair

The Gap to Salvation

They measured the body
of cloth to be hung
from here, across the gap,
to salvation.

What they saw
in their dreams
dissolved into smoke.

She began to mend
their ragged bodies
with that thick smoke
and a darning needle.
She chased away the flies
who looked to undo
her handwork.

Piles of wrinkled hills,
then fabric pooled
like soft water,
then more, hung
like the loose garments
of moss on humid trees.

What they saw
in their dreams
was a lie.

Simon Anton Niño Diego Baena

THE FUNERAL

Someone is always washing dishes
as the scent of stale perfume lingers.

And the neighbors continue jogging
with their dogs, and the leaves hang
like swollen tongues of tortured prisoners
unable to utter the names of those who perished—

No. People do not often bury their heads
                    on the pillows and weep.

                    In the room,
                    things stay as they are.

And the kid sitting on the lawn
could only fly his drone

if he ever wants to storm heaven.

Jonathan Weinert, Guest Poetry Editor

A Magnanimous Community: Some Notes on Process

In his famous 1952 book *Synchronicity*, Swiss psychiatrist C. G. Jung defined the title term as a "principle of organization" that accounts for connections among events that are not the result of cause and effect. Jung argues that the frequency of "meaningful coincidences" in many people's lives suggests an underlying order and structure to experience, a hidden network that connects everything and everyone. Without such a unifying order, life becomes "a chaotic collection of curiosities, rather like those old natural-history cabinets where one finds, cheek by jowl with fossils and anatomical monsters in bottles, the horn of a unicorn, a mandragora manikin, and a dried mermaid."

Jung meant to champion the underlying order and condemn the chaotic collection, but both notions appeal to me, and both can apply to the sequence of poems collected in this issue of *The Louisville Review*.

It's an open secret that a fair amount of chance is involved in the process of selecting poems for publication. I solicited poems from exactly one of the twenty-two poets who appear here, preferring instead to choose from the thousand or so submitted poems that I read. From my point of view, chance played a role in which poems found their way into the thousand, but something other than chance informed the selection I made out of them. Whatever you call that something other—taste, or temperament, or maybe intuition—it was chance from the point of view of the submitters, who could have had no idea that mine was the sensibility governing the selection. I had about thirty-five pages to fill, so I could accept only twenty-seven poems from the total submitted, or less than three percent. There were at least another fifty poems that could have made the cut, but chance played a role here too, as my final choices were guided by what I happened to find exciting and compelling and mysterious during the weeks I was working on the project.

Chance played no part in the sequencing, on the other hand. Like the curiosities in Jung's cabinet, I placed the poems "cheek by jowl," but in a very particular (that is to say, non-chaotic) order. I did not sequence the poems alphabetically by author, nor did I order them by author at all, such that multiple poems by the same author are sometimes adjacent to one another and sometimes not. Instead, I ordered the poems to tell a story, or to create an arc, the way one might do when putting together a book.

You will find no bottle monsters, unicorn horns, or dried mermaids in the poems offered here, but you will encounter curiosities. Underlying themes and recurring images began to emerge as I put the sequence together, and these echo and thread throughout the collection. I feel now, with the order of poems settled, that the sequence exhibits a coherent, if elusive, "principle of organization." Whether that principle points to a hidden order of the kind that Jung had in mind, or simply to the accidents of my own peculiar sensibility, I can't say. But the connections are surprising, and the correspondences are there in the poems.

Veterans of poetry workshops will recognize the odd phenomenon whereby several participants, often strangers to one another, bring in several poems on the same theme or containing the same image. One day there's a run on poems about maternal grandmothers; another day, it's spatulas or calla lilies. (Is it chance, or is there "something in the air"?) The sequence here starts with a run of poems about rooms and windows and dwelling places, beginning with Peter Grandbois' "I am done being this tiny house." Grandbois' poem is not only the first house poem, but also the first of a number of very short poems that seemed to want to bunch together, like a cluster of tiny bombs.

The Grandbois poem is in several ways initiatory, giving onto vistas both interior and exterior. It's a poem, if you will, with a lot of wind gushing through it. I encountered more than a few lyrics about life during lockdown as I went along, but I found Grandbois' oblique approach particularly haunting and effective. If the poem was in fact inspired by too many days confined to a tiny house, it has enough metaphorical heft to generate meaning long after the lockdowns have lifted and the pandemic has become an unhappy memory.

Although it occasionally slips out of sight and then resurfaces, the house/window thread winds throughout the sequence, and you can trace its progress through to the end. Simon Perchik's first untitled poem picks up the Grandbois trope of a dwelling-place open to the elements (water, in Perchik's case), and like the Grandbois poem, it lands on an image of a window. The tension between inner and outer in "I am done being this tiny house" evolves in the Perchik poem into a tension between freedom and confinement. That tension in turn drives Laurie Welch's surprising "Sonnet for the Murderous Plains." The house/window thread weaves together with other threads that are also stitched into and across the sequence, arriving in the end at the final, acerbic image in Simon Anton Diego Niño Baena's "The Funeral." The inner/outer and freedom/confinement oppositions become cosmic here, vainly straining to reconcile heaven and earth.

There are other threads. The "desire" announced in Grandbois' fourteen-word poem, for instance, opens the window for Maxima Kahn's "Meditations on Desire," an astonishing hundred-line pantoum, and the series of love-stunned poems that follow it. Kahn's poem also creates an illuminating comparison with the short poems that surround it and serves as an object lesson on how to coordinate a long poem's energies so that the ending detonates. The short poems, in contrast, are entirely detonation.

There is much more to say, but I wish to do no more here than point to the kind of stitching that went into creating the series. My hope is that discovering and following the threads yourself will please you as much as weaving them together pleased me.

So then, which of Jung's views is the more apropos: synchronicity revealing an underlying order and structure, or experience as "a collage of glitches," as Laurie Welch's poem phrases it? I lean toward the glitches, but there remains a mysterious element that chance can't account for. I sometimes imagine that poets secretly signal one another when they write, and that bringing together disparate voices exposes a hidden communications matrix that connects writers across time and space. Even if there's an element of wishful thinking in this picture, I believe that it's meaningful, and potentially practical. If nothing else, it's a way to imagine oneself into a magnanimous community in which the members are open to one another, value one another, and listen and respond to one another. Such community seems increasingly hard to come by these days, but the world needs more magnanimity now, and it needs it urgently. I hope that you will feel included in the implied community when you read the sequence of poems here, and that it contributes, in however small a way, to the sum of fellow-feeling and human affection.

Stan Lee Werlin

Hummingbird

Colm's eyes are drawn to it the moment he enters the busy auction preview. It's the only instrument he cares about, the entire reason he's there. The identification sign—Lot 12, Gibson Hummingbird, 1965— is clearly visible at the far end of the room. The guitar itself rests on a simple upright display stand, the light reflecting off the polished rosewood and the crimson pick guard with the flowers etched in white. The long uncut ends of the six metal strings notched in the guitar's tuning clamps are easily visible as they fly off in all directions like the strands of a wispy wild hairdo, the thick ribbed gold of the bass strings arcing and looping against the smooth thin silver of the trebles. He can almost hear the quiet metallic sounds a microphone would pick up in the midst of an accomplished player's riff or energetic strumming as they scrape and bounce off each other.

Colm's personal assistant trolls the internet daily for upcoming sales of classic guitars. She searches for estate sales and auctions, reviewing their item listings and catalogues meticulously. She scans updates on new arrivals posted by a long list of the leading music stores that specialize in serving the needs of guitar aficionados and collectors. They all know about his unique needs. On the hunt for more than twenty years, he has talked to every one of the major sellers, pleading with them to call him the moment they might have acquired what he's looking for. The online catalogue descriptions of vintage guitars being sold in an estate auction, she discovered only the previous afternoon, included among the several Hummingbirds listed one in particular with vaguely promising language—*This guitar features unusual personal artwork*. It's the reason he left his brief unfinished, lurched out of the office for two unplanned vacation days and grabbed an overnight flight from Los Angeles to Boston.

Colm remembers the aptitude testing all those years ago with a mixture of shame and deep-seated feelings of inadequacy. His Ivy-educated parents took it on blind faith that their genetics would endow him with ample intelligence. They were concerned instead with pushing him to develop the non-academic skills of a "well-rounded" student: athletics, music, art, creative writing.

"Colm," his father announces one bright Saturday morning when he's eight years old and wants nothing more than to be out biking in the neighborhood with his friends, "Mom and I invited two people here today to give you a few fun tests. They're coming soon to go to the playground with us."

They take him to the field at a nearby school to assess gross motor skills and coordination. He sits at the desk in his bedroom for a battery of tests that involve manual dexterity. White hot tears streak his face when he feels humiliated by his fumbling inability to fit a set of colorful oddly-shaped objects into a panel of equally oddly-shaped receptacles.

He's closeted away in his room sullen and sulking when the testers sum it up to his parents that same afternoon, well out of Colm's earshot. "Mechanical aptitude: nil. Artistic vision and skills: minimal. Ability to see in three dimensions: very limited. Solid geometry will pose difficulties. Not likely to succeed as an engineer. Athletic prowess: average, though Colm is a strong, fast runner and exhibits excellent hand-eye coordination at the gross level. Fine motor skills: exceptional, possibly gifted. The testing did not assess musical skills. Recommendations: Colm is best suited to baseball. He would probably be a better than average batter, and a sure-handed infielder. Tennis might be a good second choice. He is likely to develop proficiency with a stringed musical instrument such as guitar or banjo if well-motivated."

In the months that follow, Colm's father, a man who disdains athletics and was never an athlete himself, refuses—despite Colm's howling protests—to let him play Little League baseball. Both parents enjoy classical music; the house is filled with the sound of thunderous symphonic crescendos and quietly delicate concertos on weekend mornings to which Colm remains indifferent. Still, his mother pleads her case for two months running. "How about the violin or cello? I learned on your grandfather's violin. It's a family heirloom. We'll get it tuned up for you." Colm agrees instead on an inexpensive starter guitar and weekly lessons. It's not his top priority, but he keeps at it and slowly masters the basics.

Colm surveys the auction floor. He walks casually down a crowded aisle featuring classic Martins, stopping to admire a D-35 that appears as new and untouched as it might have looked when he bought his Hummingbird all those years ago.

"Beautiful instrument, isn't it? I assume you play?" A fortyish, well dressed and immaculately groomed millennial holds out his hand. "Scott Palmer. I know most of the collectors in this area, but I don't think we've met, have we? Me, I'm here for the Martins. There must be, what, at least forty beauties on display? Something for everyone I hope."

Colm offers Scott a firm handshake. "Colm Davidson. And yes, I play, though truthfully the last time was almost fifty years ago in a college folk music trio. I'm not sure my fingers would even remember a half dozen chords now. Just learned about this auction and flew in overnight from L.A. The Martins are first class, absolutely, but I'm more of a Gibson man. Looking for just the right vintage Hummingbird." When he takes a step back to admire the Martin in front of them, Scott gives him a surprised stare.

"Wait, I don't understand. You took a redeye flight from L.A. to get to this auction just to see the Hummingbirds? But you can find them all over the web. All the major dealers sell them, pack and ship ultra-carefully, satisfaction guaranteed. You know that I'm sure. Four, five, maybe six thousand bucks and you can usually find one in excellent condition. Or wait a few weeks and another one will show up for sale. So why get on a plane and fly all this way?"

Colm lifts his eyes from the Martin and looks off in the distance, a bemused smile on his face as he conjures up a private memory. "I'm not in the market for just any vintage Hummingbird, Scott. I'm hoping to find it in pristine condition, sure, but it won't matter even if it's beaten up. I'm looking for the Irish Cassie."

When he walks through the door of Boston's largest guitar store on a busy winter Saturday just after turning sixteen, Colm is completely overwhelmed by the dozens of acoustic instruments on display and the resonant sounds that surround him from the buyers playing in every aisle. He's been swept up in the rising tide of social consciousness and the flourishing singer-songwriter movement, and he's determined to make a difference. The lyrics of political awareness and activism—the "protest" songs of the folk music genre—are going mainstream, successfully muscling in for radio airtime right alongside the songs chronicling teen love and tortured relationships, fast cars, and surfing. He worships at the feet of Phil Ochs, Bob Dylan, Peter Paul & Mary. He'll learn to finger-pick on an instrument worthy of his vision. Form a duo or trio when he gets to college. Devote himself to writing songs.

He spends the morning trying out the pricy Martins and Epiphones, but it's the stunning visual appeal of the Gibsons that finally draws him in. The Dove and the J-series impress him, but if it's possible to fall in love with an inanimate object, that's pretty much what happens when he picks up a Hummingbird.

He'll have to drain his savings account to buy this guitar, but it's decided in just minutes. To Colm, every detail of design reflects perfection: the cherry sunburst finish, the mahogany body, the rosewood fingerboard perfect for the size of his hand. The square-shoulder dreadnought shape sets it apart from the other acoustics. The double parallelogram silver inlays on the frets add class, as do the gold tuning pegs. The sound when he strums a chord is exquisitely rich and the reverb of the bass breathtaking. But for some reason it's the artistic design of the oversized crimson-colored pick guard with its single hummingbird hovering above a white trumpet flower, its long beak and tongue probing for nectar, that seals the deal. He's no artist, but this—somehow this is special. By the time he gets the guitar home, he's never felt more committed to anything.

Even before Colm's through his first semester at Boston University, he's already deeply embedded in the world of concerts and coffeehouses in Boston and Cambridge. The ad in the monthly rag *Broadside* that chronicles the explosion of the folk music scene locally and nationally leaps off the page. Guitar lessons from Ted Mandell, the well-known studio accompanist for several leading artists! He sees it as his breakthrough.

He rides the T to Harvard Square in a fit of nervous energy, running through the streets to the address Ted gave him, his guitar case flailing wildly at his side. The January cold is bracing, the sidewalks slushy and slippery from a snow that has just ended, and when he skids and loses his balance the case crashes to the sidewalk and bounces awkwardly off a parking meter stanchion. Muted notes generated by the collision sound briefly inside the case as he regains his footing. He rushes up the stairs to the second-floor apartment when Ted buzzes him in.

A tall, thin goateed man welcomes him with a powerful handshake. It's surprisingly warm inside. "You must be Colm. I'm Ted Mandell." Ted looks to be in his late twenties and fits the caricature of a counterculture hippie in every way Colm can imagine. His blond hair is stringy and disheveled; he's barefoot, and unmistakably high on weed. The scent of marijuana permeates the air and is heavy and cloying in the large living room. He wears a tie-dyed short sleeve shirt revealing toned, muscular arms. Colm's eyes are drawn to his hands, the length of his fingers, the nails on his right hand particularly thick and smooth. His picking hand, Colm realizes. Clothing is strewn on a side chair and on a tattered couch where two acoustic guitars rest. Two more guitars perch on stands near a wide bay window that looks out onto a quiet alley and across the street to a row of unremarkable brown and gray three-deckers with cars jammed haphazardly into their unplowed driveways. There's even a lute off in a corner.

Colm glances at the half-open door to a bedroom at the other end of the room. He catches sight of a lithe and decidedly naked and smooth-skinned woman rising gracefully off a large mattress on the floor as a man's hand reaches out and the door quickly swings shut. Ted's laughing as he tells Colm the names of his guests and Colm goes wide-eyed with recognition. "Maybe you'll meet them later," Ted says. "We're putting together a new song to intro at their concert tomorrow. In the meantime, maybe you want a toke before we get started? Let's see your guitar." Drugs are still a whole new world to Colm and he feels sheepish declining the dope. While he opens his case and picks up his Hummingbird, Ted takes a deep draw on the tiny remains of a joint. "Okay, show me what you can do. You can use yours or mine." He points to one of the guitars lying on the couch. "That one's in open D tuning. The one next to it is open G. Back there in the corner, B flat modal. So impress me, throw in some harmonics."

Colm can't even think how to respond. Ted might just as well have asked him to solve an advanced calculus problem involving partial differential equations. He can play all the basic chords, has a modest proficiency finger-picking, a good sense of rhythm for strumming. He knows some of the easier chord progressions. But tunings? Harmonics? His embarrassment is acute.

"Well right now I'm in a duo playing with another guy in my dorm. Colm and Cal, maybe you've seen us? We play open mic nights mostly. We do this one a lot." He starts to play "Don't Think Twice, It's All Right", flubbing a few transitions, swallowing words as he sings. Halfway through, Ted picks up a guitar and improvises an accompaniment. "You could do this," he says, playing a quick riff. "Or this. Or this." What's meant to encourage Colm only serves to underscore the limitations of his playing.

When Colm stops, Ted plays the distinctive backup of a popular song by a rapidly rising female singer-songwriter Colm admires. His fingers fly across the frets in combinations Colm has never seen. "I worked this one out with her right here and then we hit the studio."

"I have a long way to go, don't I?' Colm says. "I guess I'm not really blessed with a ton of musical talent." Colm finds himself wishing those testers back when he was eight had known his IQ for sharps and flats and keys was non-existent and had never suggested his parents steer him in a musical direction.

"Let's try to jam," Ted says. "Listen to what I'm playing for twenty seconds and then join in. Watch my hand on the fretboard to get the chords, but don't replicate what I'm doing. I want to see something from you that complements my piece." Colm tries to keep up, but everything he does sounds wrong, out of sync, disharmonious. Hi glassy-eyed look tells all.

Ted's sympathetic. "We'll just work on memorizing how to finger-pick specific songs. Kind of a brute force approach. You can do that on your own, though. If I can, I'll help you become a knowledgeable, musically creative player. If you don't make progress along those lines, there's no point in working with me. Fair enough?"

"Fair enough."

Ted lays out his first assignment. "Come back with a Renaissance-style version of 'Where Have All the Flowers Gone'. Be creative!" Ted plays a gavotte right out of the Middle Ages to inspire Colm as he packs up and leaves.

Colm works tirelessly on his piece, but it just sounds dull and plodding the following week when he plays it for Ted. "I worked so hard to make it flowing and relaxing. But it's just clunky and uninteresting, isn't it?" Ted has to agree. They work together at improving it for a full hour. Ted knocks off one improvisation after another to show Colm the range of possibilities, while Colm struggles to eke out a few worthy bars. He realizes there's no point in continuing.

"Maybe I'll see you and Cal at a show somewhere around," Ted says. "If you ever want to sell that Hummingbird, let me know. I'd take it off your hands in a heartbeat."

Cal's the better guitarist anyway, Colm thinks as he walks down the stairwell to the street and rides the T back to BU. *He can do the highlight solos. I'll focus on writing the songs.*

Colm and Cal are on stage singing the last song of their set at The Unicorn's weekly open mic night. They're both long and lanky, clean-shaven, no freshman fifteen swelling their firm flat abs. Their close-fitting tees and jeans suggest athleticism, though neither is interested in sports. Right now Colm's mind is no longer on the song and he almost misses the lyrics. His eyes are fixated on the wafer thin blonde in the Simmons sweatshirt who's been sitting alone at a tiny front row table directly at their feet. When she stands up to sway to the driving beat of the tune and sing along, he's beguiled by her impossibly wide smile and dancing blue eyes and straight nearly white hair that reaches her waist. He wonders if she dyes and irons it to get that look. He leans over and whispers to Cal who winks and nods as the song ends. They get a smattering of applause from the sparse Monday crowd they're used to seeing, and Colm steps down off the stage to take the open chair at her table as Cal quietly disappears.

"First time seeing us?" he asks. "Really hope you liked what you heard. I'm Colm Davidson."

"You guys need a woman's voice if you're going to get anywhere," she says. There's no preamble, she's just out there with it. For some reason, Colm's attracted to that directness. When she extends her hand, the spark he feels when he touches it is magnetic, and he's reluctant to let go. "Cassie Wilson. Where'd your partner go? Let's go try a few songs together. You'll see what I mean." She lets her fingers linger in his. The spark is definitely mutual.

They walk to Colm and Cal's BU dorm near Kenmore Square. As soon as they start singing they know that she's right. Their voices mesh effortlessly. It's easy to see how their personalities will play off each other on stage. They instantly like each other. Cal can see that romance will bloom between Colm and Cassie but he doesn't think it will matter and anyway, the music's the most important thing. They stay up all night playing with harmonies and arrangements and by the time the sun rises they all know that they're a trio.

"We need a name," Cassie says. "Something catchy. How about 'The Flowers Gone'?" She sings a line from the song. *Where have all the flowers gone, long time passing?*

"The Flowers Gone?" Cal questions. "A little prissy fancy artsy, isn't it? Maybe turn that around. Gone To Flowers." *Where have all the graveyards gone? Gone to flowers, every one.*

Colm jumps in. "We're already playing as Colm and Cal. That's our identity. We shouldn't get away from it. So how about 'Colm, Cal and Cassie'? Easy to remember. Great alliteration. Keeps it personal." Cal and Cassie agree. 'Colm, Cal and Cassie' it is.

Cassie's standing behind Colm again, kneading his shoulder muscles while he sits at his desk working on the lyrics of another song. Sometimes she's unnaturally still as she peers over him to study what he's writing. At other times he senses her pulsating with energy like a hummingbird hovering in the summer air at a mimosa or a butterfly bush, flitting quickly from flower to flower. When she does this, she tests out one possible melody after another, humming softly but insistently and always into Colm's left ear. She distracts him when she breathes into that ear, kissing and nibbling his earlobe. There's something distinctive about the hovering and the humming, something fierce and determined and uniquely Cassie. He likes it so much that he starts calling her *Hummingbird*, then just *Bird*, a name she finds affectionate and endearing. He tries *Hummy* once and she shoves him hard in the chest and narrows her eyes in a piercing glare. *Birdie* elicits an even more violent reaction, as if the name evokes disdain and condescension. She finds it distasteful. But *Bird? Bird* she likes.

"Bird, stop," he implores as her hands reach down to press gently against his chest, her fingers drawing slow, tight circles there as her lips whisper against his neck. "C'mon, let me finish the last stanza." She wants him urgently in the bedroom, not penning another song that earns them the half-hearted applause they've come to accept as the constant disappointing measure of their popularity. "Later," she says, tugging on his shirt impatiently until he mock-sighs and the last line of the stanza eludes him as they fall in a heap on the bed.

In two years, the trio goes nowhere. They're off campus, living together with Cal and three other roommates in a dingy three bedroom apartment. The heady sense of freedom is exhilarating, almost spiritual, though freewheeling togetherness hasn't boosted their musical progress or popularity at all. The initial sense of euphoria—*Colm, Cal and Cassie*—they thought the syllabic symmetry to their idols Peter, Paul and Mary would somehow help—is long gone. When they play gigs, they emulate PP&M's stage presence. They change positions smoothly after every song, glance knowingly at each other's eyes, lean toward each other to bring their heads together at the microphone as if doing so will enhance their appeal. When they sing, Cassie even tries to bob her head and flick her waist-long hair back and forth the same way Mary captures attention, but her hair's too long and the repeated gesture looks awkward and forced.

They've got some talent, but so do dozens of other would-be performers. Colm works hard at the songwriting. They've got a few originals that audiences appreciate, but his voice is serviceable, nothing more. Cal's singing isn't much better. Cassie's the musically gifted one. She can hear the melodies in her head almost as soon as Colm gets the lyrics on paper. Her voice commands attention and dominates the trio's sound. They mix covers of popular folk songs with their own originals at open mics and anti-war rallies and at the hootenannies at the many local colleges. They dream of a breakthrough at a big name coffeehouse and audition repeatedly for an offer to open for a headliner at The Unicorn, Club 47, and several others. The long string of turndowns is disappointing and frustrating and takes a toll.

The Irish Cassie? Scott's face puckers in puzzlement. Colm answers the next question even before Scott can frame it aloud. "I bought it new in 1965, played it for six years before I sold it in '71. The name, the Irish Cassie—well, you'll see why if I find it here today. Been searching for more than twenty years. A fool's errand, I imagine you're thinking. Ridiculous odds stacked against me. And that's true, nothing but dead ends so far. Still, unless it was somehow destroyed or literally thrown away in the trash, it's out there somewhere. They only manufactured about 1200 that year, so when one shows up it's worth chasing. Sure, maybe a few get passed down as family heirlooms. But all the others— sooner or later they come to market. Vintage guitars are a lucrative business. I can't cover every last vendor, auction, collector, and internet sale, but I'm trying."

"So you're looking for your own Hummingbird? A guitar you haven't touched in fifty years? But why? It must be costing you a ton of time and a small fortune. What's the draw?"

"Memories, Scott, simple as that. This guitar, it'll bring back a special time in my life. I'm huge on nostalgia. I think a lot of us boomers are. My unsentimental friends tell me I live in the past, but I'm OK with that.

"Cassie was the girl in that college trio I mentioned. If this guitar is the one I owned, we'll drink, I'll tell you stories about her. Let's go see if twenty years of frustration is about to end. You might need to run a little interference."

Cassie has a plan. As soon as Colm heads out for his long Wednesday class schedule, she yanks Cal out of bed. Colm won't return until early evening. "Cal, I need you to take the strings out of the Hummingbird." "What? Cass, what are you going to do? Don't mess with Colm's guitar. He'll be furious if you do something flaky."

"Please, Cal, just do it. Don't worry, I'm not going to break anything. And Cal? I work fast. I'll be done in a few hours. Get the strings in before Colm gets back, okay? I want him to be surprised."

Cassie pulls out her acrylic paints and her fine detail paintbrushes and lays them out on their living room worktable. She's an art history major and a talented artist in her own right. Their walls are covered with portraits of Cal and Colm, self-portraits, the trio on stage at the different venues they play. Her delicate watercolors and vivid alcohol inks and charcoals are striking. After Cal removes the strings, she opens a tube of sealant and gets to work.

One glance at the guitar is all it takes the next morning. "Bird! Bird! Bird!" Colm yelps when he sees that two small hummingbirds outlined in white have joined the artwork on the pick guard near the trumpet flowers at the bridge. "Bird, what the fuck? You drew on my guitar? What were you thinking?"

"Take it easy, Col. Now there's a trio of birds. Like the three of us. It's just, I don't know, just a creative touch I thought might bring us better luck." Colm's mollified easily when Cassie gives him a quick hug and smiles and just shrugs her shoulders like it's no big deal. And it isn't. He knows she hasn't done any damage, and she's right, they definitely need a break to go their way. Maybe they'll find inspiration from her artwork. It's not until two nights later when he breaks a string on stage and decides to install a fresh set that Colm discovers the rest of what Cassie has done.

Colm is single-mindedly focused as he and Scott weave their way across the scuffed hardwood floor through the growing crowd. He's moving in a fit of anticipatory joy, holding his breath, brushing past people, avoiding eye contact. Could it possibly be the one? At long last, could it be the one? When he reaches it, he grasps the neck halfway down while his mind stretches back fifty years to the first time he touched his Hummingbird and placed a capo on its frets. He lifts it off the guitar stand as Scott steps calmly into the path of an attendant who's rushing over and shouting, "Sir! Only visual examination of items is allowed, no touching. Can't you read?" Colm ignores the obvious posted prohibition. He stares closely at the pick guard. Its surface is worn to dullness and covered with dozens of deep, violent scratches, almost as if it had been deliberately abused. He searches for the telltale markings he hopes to see, Cassie's two hummingbirds, but they're not there. Still, he knows they could easily have worn off or flaked away over the years. And who knows if it's even the original. Pick guards can be replaced. Besides, the pick guard isn't what's important to him.

They play their last gig a week before graduation. They've seen it coming for most of the year already, the music waning, their appearances more infrequent, their future pathways looming ever closer. Cal's deciding among business schools. Colm's heading to law school in L.A. For months Cassie has feigned indecision, casually dismissed questions and carefully closed off talk about what's next for her. Colm just assumes she will follow him west and he isn't prepared for the gut-punch conversation with her that blindsides him and leaves him feeling utterly weightless and unmoored.

"Wait, Bird, you're not coming with me? I don't understand. You're not coming? I thought, I just thought…" Colm trails off. He's unable to think as he tries to control the welling nausea and the accelerating feeling of betrayal that's overwhelming his senses.

Cassie's never thought about a future with Colm. She realizes that she hardly knows who she is, not nearly enough for commitment or permanence to be important in that future. She knows this with unshakable clarity, the same way she knows her own name. "It's been great, Col, it has. But I need to let go. I feel myself constantly changing. There are days I wake up and know I'll never again be who I was the day before. I feel like ever since I've known you I've been spinning a chrysalis and I still have no idea who'll emerge. All I really know is that I need to be free to go wherever the Cassie I'm becoming takes me."

Colm stands silent, as speechless as if his tongue has been ripped from his mouth and he'll never talk again. He looks at Cassie for what seems like forever until words finally come. Is she holding back any sadness at all? She must be, Colm thinks. She must be. He knows that arguing would be pointless, anger antagonistic, bitterness immature, but he can't help himself. "Well you know what, Bird?" He spits out her name venomously. He's never done that before, never, and it shocks him to hear his heated tone. "You know what? After everything we've done together and meant to each other? I guess you're really just that girl in the Joni Mitchell song we sing who won't let herself be tied down. Aren't you? Aren't you? Aren't you?" He throws his hands in the air and helplessly punches his thighs again and again in a futile effort to punish himself for his lovestruck blindness and naïve expectations. Finally, he picks up his guitar and strums the melody while he chokes out the words Cassie sings when they perform. *He will find it hard to shake her from his memory, while she's off somewhere being free.* He stops playing as abruptly as he started. "That's me. That's you. That's us." And it is. And Bird flies.

The Hummingbird begins a journey of its own a week later. From Colm to Ted, from Ted to a string of temperamental players, eventually leaving the folk world and coming to rest with The Rolling Stones. They use it on tour for acoustic numbers until they unload it to a London guitar broker who holds it well over a decade before he eventually extracts a small fortune from a wealthy Boston-based collector who's convinced that its provenance as a "Stones-used" instrument makes it a rare prize. It sits in the collector's display room for many more years with several dozen other rare guitars until the executors of his will in their haste upon his death entirely overlook the paperwork that establishes the Hummingbird's value and arrange for an estate sale, to which Colm, thanks to his alert assistant, has just now found his way.

Colm ignores the angry auction attendant and with a conspiratorial grin at Scott he pulls a small flashlight from his pocket. He thrusts his face toward the sound hole and angles the light through the strings as he peers into the guitar, searching for the image drawn on the light interior wood that will mean the Hummingbird he once cherished and has been hunting against all odds has returned to his hands. When he lifts his eyes away from the guitar and looks at Scott, his body is trembling. He doesn't know whether to laugh or weep or even if can remember how to breathe.

"Colm?"

Colm hands him the guitar. "See for yourself, Scott."

The image Scott sees is a young woman's face and unclothed upper back. Her torso is turned to the viewer at an angle so that her face gazes over her shoulder through the sound hole as if staring directly at anyone looking in at her. Her features are exquisitely delicate against fair light skin: Nordic blue eyes slightly almond-shaped, a short narrow nose, high well-defined cheekbones, tight thin lips parting to reveal a hint of her tongue and teeth. Her hair flows in long pink tresses down her back, a color so unusual that it immediately draws Scott's attention. Her head is tilted at a downward angle and the look in her eyes, combined with just the suggestion of a winsome smile, is undeniably sultry and coquettish and beckoning.

"So this is it, Colm? You've really found it?"

"It's Cassie, Scott. It's Cassie. I was crazy about her. The only girl I ever loved. That's her face. She got Cal to take out the strings one day when she knew I'd be gone to classes and this is what she did. She was such a talented artist. She was a blonde, though. Her hair was so fine and white that when the stage lights reflected off her it was almost blinding. I can still hear what she said when I discovered what she'd drawn inside the guitar. *You told me once you favored the Irish girls. Fair pale skin with a few freckles and always that lustrous red hair. Said you'd faint dead away if I could look like that. So here you go, you've got your Irish Cassie now.* The hair was a deep orange-red when she drew it but I guess over all the years it's had plenty of time to fade to pink. That's her. That's my Cassie. That's my Bird."

Colm hands the guitar to the floor attendant who carefully returns it to its display stand. His body feels electrified, limbs tingling with nervous energy as he and Scott take seats together, waiting for the bidding to begin. Just before the auctioneer steps up to the podium and tap-tests the microphone, Scott nudges Colm on the shoulder. "So what happened? Cassie, I mean."

"All through school I thought we would be together forever. But by the time senior year rolled around I guess she started having other ideas. Free. She wanted to be free. I was blind not to see it. She went off to an artist's commune in the Oregon wilderness. Probably found a swami or a tantric yoga master or a Zen guru offering the true counterculture experience. Drugs. Free love. A quest for the peace that passeth all understanding. After law school, I wound up married to my work. For all I know she could still be up in those mountains somewhere. Whatever she wanted, I hope she found it."

"Did you write each other love letters when you were together?"

"Love letters?" Colm shakes his head. "No, that wasn't our thing," he says, squinting at Scott quizzically as if to ask where that question came from. "That just wasn't our thing."

"And after? Did you ever, you know, try to find her?"

"I actually thought about it when I finished law school. But no. Three years had passed. She knew where I was for those three years and I never heard a word from her. What would have been the point?"

Scott purses his lips and nods. He turns his attention back to the auctioneer. Colm doesn't have to tell him his quest isn't really about the music, or the guitar. That's just a shaped wooden body and a well-constructed neck and attachments for securing and tuning the strings. He's certain that Colm isn't going to play the Hummingbird or even put his fingers on the frets to form a chord. He's doing something far more meaningful. Love letters come in many forms. He's reclaiming the only one Cassie ever gave him.

The lots are moving along briskly. Soon they hear the announcement, "Lot 12, the 1965 Gibson Hummingbird." Someone brings the guitar forward to center stage and the bidding begins. The auctioneer is frenzied as he urges the bids higher. Colm raises his paddle again and again and again. He can almost feel Cassie leaning over his shoulder in their college apartment, testing out a new melody, humming the music of her heart fiercely into his ear. In his mind he sees the trio on a coffeehouse stage, earnest and aspiring as he and Cassie crowd the microphone on their signature duet, their faces so close together they might suddenly steal a kiss that draws smiles and murmurs and even applause from the audience. Cassie's breath is sweet and pure and intoxicating as it mingles with his own. "Oh Bird," he whispers. "Oh Bird."

J. A. Bernstein

Musclewood

In the dream, the dream that is life, the valley is lit from below: a golden sun hovers beyond the burning grass, a spiny silhouette of hemlock, white pines, and black oak. The whole place feels magical, this does, and she recalls being here in a dream.

Except it's *now*, and she's not.

Sunday, July 19, 2020. Grand Mere State Park, southwestern Michigan. She's come with her husband and three kids, having escaped the heat and confinement that is life for them in Mississippi during the plague. She's returned to her childhood haunt, if only for another week. Her younger daughter thunders down from a dune, hands waving, teeth clenched, a fine spray of silt churning up from the wake at her heels. Somewhere, another child cries, or possibly laughs. What difference does it make, she begins to concede, in this glowing expanse of green woods, with the blue herons cawing throatily, the prairie warblers awash in their bunchberry stems, the rock jasmine cracking in wind?

She can smell hyacinths, the musclewood trees, the sunscreen her daughter sweats off.

She recalls having sledded here once as a girl. *Was it a dream?*

Her husband says their youngest ran off. The boy's tumbling through panic grass, or so his giggles say. A cricket frog ticks from South Lake.

She believes she should chase him—her son, not the frog. A quiet sun clusters the pines. She can feel the wind changing—this night, silent breeze.

She's forty-one, here with her clan. And she should feel connection to her husband, to her kids and this world, but all she can sense is herself: the quiet dignity of living, of smelling grass plains, the whorled mountain mint casting white blooms, the bald rush.

She can see herself sledding, a girl of four, five, her oily Flexible Flyer creaking like a meadowlark's breast as she passes through whiteness, this blank open space, and the sky opens up, and she goes…

Jessica Evans

The repair was supposed to be temporary; maybe the marriage

was too

A faded green cookbook half in French because she dreamed of being something more back when her bank teller job led her into the shop where he worked selling sheet music. A little girl clutched at her hand and knew immediately the man with slick smiles would destroy her mother.

Thick flour dusted pages, dogeared and splotched with sauces and gravies when she worked so hard to create something magnificent, her family now grown. The old oven handle broke last winter and now she has to use a stick to keep the door closed. There's a metaphor there, she's sure of it, but doesn't have time to unravel her losses or her longings. A deep notch cut into the top is in the shape of a V but this is no victory. Elise wipes her hands on her apron, one of the few things left from her life before.

Sometimes the ingredients are too expensive, unattainable, so she spends Sunday mornings, cigarette burning in the ashtray, dreaming about another life. Canapes and crudités, the sort of entertaining that would need silver and crystal, linen, and influence. Piecemealed and no longer whole, what remains of her silver tea set sits on a window sill, cold to touch in winter, flatlined and blank in summer.

The oven stick was supposed to be temporary but it's worn a hole through the linoleum, exposing the rough patch of resin and limestone underneath. When Elise is drunk enough not to see the decay collecting in the corners of her life, she pretends the patch is portal to somewhere better. A family seated at a round oak table, its thick center column support enough for her hope.

Leslie Daniels

HOUSE MAGIC

She's driving to her friend's house, the porch in her mind, intending to sit in the wicker rocker overlooking the garden and ask a question. Her friend is the marrying kind, and she is not. She hopes to ask if she should marry the man she's been dating. Peonies will be blooming at their feet, *a bevy of blowzy beauties*, she thinks, having read too many mediocre novels of the twentieth century, with their mistrals of misogyny.

What she'll ask instead is *What's the strangest thing you believe?*

At her friend's house the improbable is true. The road to her house is itself a vortex. On it she sometimes disappears and reemerges, having passed her destination.

She thinks about the date last night, his birthday. She'd hoped to go dancing, but instead they went to a restaurant with high ceilings. Buildings interest him, their use and structure. In his mind people come and go, she suspects, like flitting swallows. "This place was a hospital," he said of the restaurant, "I was born here in this wing."

This fact takes away her appetite. No oysters wrapped in bacon, no sip of Prosecco will bring it back.

This could be love, she thinks. Or not.

Still driving to her friend's porch, on the road that now stretches the width of the county, she thinks of the first wedding she attended, a hippy affair at a commune in Powelton Village. Her young parents had taken her there with her sister.

A man in an upstairs bedroom offered them pot. "I'm twelve," she'd said, not wanting to be rude, but indignant nonetheless. The joint was burning in his pinched fingers. Downstairs people were sitting on the floor, passing jugs of wine. None wore fancy clothes, not even the bride. There was talk of love. People wept. No one's parents were there except hers. She remembers an immense amount of hair, long and curly, beard hair, fros white and black, scarves and flowers twined through hair. She'd been expecting a wedding from books: pretty clothes and formality, decorum, the show at least of elegance. In the commune, people were activists against the war, for racial justice; civil disobedience warriors making history. She'd felt her distance from them. *I will not be this kind* of grownup. I will not live in a commune or marry in a long green dress with flowers in my hair. This is not my story.

She's been back to that house recently for her father's wake. Everyone was still there, but old. The ones who'd gone to jail had become lawyers and professors. They all had better haircuts, better clothes. In that house they'd shaped history. She couldn't identify the man who'd offered her the joint. By now his life would be filled with bad choices, she figures, each one stupider than the last: *Have some drugs, children.* Greeting their old faces, she reflected that if she had smoked that joint, fallen asleep in that upstairs bedroom, and slept till now, history could not have made any less sense.

She will sit on her friend's porch and she will not be dissuaded from marrying the man she's dating, the one who dances so fine, will not even ask the question. Instead she will listen to the things her friend believes, each so strange and yet reflected in the view from the porch: the teetering trees that never fall, the complex social pairings of the chickens, the kindness of the bees and the rooster.

She'll tell her friend of a different date with a different man and a different porch where she knelt, pulling weeds. What she'd wanted to communicate to him with her body is *See how useful I am? How practical?* But instead what her body said is *I don't belong here.* She tells her friend how after the weeds, but during that same evening, there was the sense of an ending, not as in I will never see you again, because in life those rarely happen. There is always five years later when someone has entered *the Program* and is making their ponderous and unwelcome amends, or the next decade when their selfish child is at the kindergarten open-house, hogging the snacks. But one of these goodbyes: this is all there is and all there will ever be. She tells her friend what she believes, that you can fractal each relationship, and kneeling on the porch, pulling weeds was a piece of nothing, a chip off the big old nothing.

Her friend is not one to talk you out of a marriage. Which she knows or she would not have come.

Later there will be the baby. She'll be living in the man's house above what used to be a dance hall.

She'll walk up those stairs, home from the hospital, holding an infant boy. She's wearing an awful dress, waffle weave gray. Her underwear is sodden, and her sandals are dusty. The tiny baby in her arms is not cute, but thin and worrisome. He has a name of his father's choosing.

The dog is overjoyed to see them. She's nervous too. Her master has brought her the infant's blanket from the hospital to smell. He is all of their masters. The woman doesn't know this yet.

At the moment she's thinking, *Well, this is the end of dancing.* Or else she's thinking, *Good thing I brought all of my underpants here.*

What she's not thinking is *I am a mother.* The baby came six weeks early and she is not ready to be a mother. Although she's thirty-five.

It's hot and his sticky little body is glued to her arms. He may be sleeping, but the difference between sleeping and waking isn't much. She thought this would be more interesting somehow, and less frightening.

She could drink a barrel of lemonade, she thinks. Or anything really, except coffee. Anything clear and cold and wet.

His boring little self is continuously asleep, eyes disappointingly closed. She thought she'd know better who is in there, but she doesn't.

The most important thing she knows about life in this moment is that her solo turn is over. Also, that she can't leave, she can never walk out that door.

She resents the presence of the dog, who smells bad.

Neither does she want the master. Never has she wanted a master.

She doesn't know if she wanted the baby, but she must have because there he is.

If she was honest with herself, she'd married the man because she liked the way he danced. Never boring and never out of rhythm.

But that's still far ahead.

The light is fading outside the car windows. Along the ditches, daisies glow white against the night.

Far ahead is her understanding: *I am the genetic boulder through which his family stream had to pass. I blocked the bad stuff. Fuck that, my DNA said to his. And fuck that too.* Her main contribution to her son's life will be the absence of obligation.

The boy grows up as if struck by lightning. Lightning on his wavy long hair, his endless back. Lightning is his speed, is in his mind and on his face. *I am the blackened stump left behind. I was once the tallest place, the place through which he came to earth.*

On the way back from her friend's house, as the light goes to black and the daisies blink out, the road now the length of night, stars rushing past overhead, she stops the car and steps out. Behind her the metal ticks and pings as it cools. She cups her hands over her eyes, then removes them, testing for absolute darkness. She feels the uprightness of her body, filled with sap like a young shoot, connecting her to whatever would be.

Donna Gay Anderson

TRIO

The young woman drove through the steamy August morning in Louisiana pointed in the direction of her future, one that would take root in Mississippi, at college, in a dorm room, in her most comfy sweatpants. It was all so intimidating, but the cushion of belongings that surrounded her in the car felt soft, familiar, reassuring. The five miles behind her were already a distant memory. One hundred twenty miles to go. 69.5 miles per hour. Alexander Hamilton and Aaron Burr sang her a lullaby through the car's speakers and it sounded like a warm blanket. In the car behind her two men followed, both stoic yet solemn in their enthusiasm about the journey. Her father commanded the wheel while her stepfather of fifteen years sat in the passenger's seat staring ahead at the girl's tail lights. Both were silent, which was comfortable. Since the girl's mother had unexpectedly died three years ago, so much had been said over and over and over. The men had nothing new to add and neither wanted to rehash the old stuff again. The girl knew they were full of trepidation, not because they were afraid for her and not because they philosophically opposed her leaving home. What they felt was more complex than either of those things. It was the pain from the chord of her childhood being cut and fashioned into a neat bow that stung a bit. It was also the foreboding of days and nights without her in their midst, constantly texting or calling or asking for permission and money and very rarely but sometimes…advice. The advice calls were the toughest and each man found himself responding to her pleas for wisdom with a "have you asked your dad?" or "have you asked your stepdad?" Fortunately, the girl had practiced enough good sense to find respectable older women to confront with conundrums of general health, sex, haircuts, undergarments, make-up and boys…who were stupid. Still, she always sought out the two men for the serious stuff, the life stuff like what Christianity should really look like and what was for dinner.

The gloom the fathers wore on their faces was mercifully out of eyeshot since she was driving in front of them. She knew she would miss them both terribly, but she also knew that she was ready for a taste of independence and uncomfortable joy. The girl was barely a teenager when her mother so unexpectedly passed away, and since that day the two men had found comfort and support in her and strangely in each other. The three of them had become a spring clover, three leaves attached by a single stem; the love and life of her mother. It would have made perfect sense for the men to see less of each other after the mother died but conversely, they had joined forces and resources to assure the girl a stable loving family even without the matriarch in place.

Tuesday nights had become family dinner night at her father's house, him cooking, a good thing because her stepdad mercifully never even attempted that part. He would contribute of course, picking up either a pie or a loaf of fresh bread from the local bakery, but cooking was not his role.

Well into Mississippi now, the girl noticed for the first time the change in topography as she drove on, due north. The ground seemed less swampy than it had thirty minutes before. The wall of trees seemed taller and the bugs hitting the windshield seemed less furious. One hundred miles to go as the men behind her took turns adjusting the air conditioner and the radio. In her mind the girl perused her new collection of masks: one with the logo of her new school, one with a giant pair of lips that laughed when you popped the pleats open, one sprinkled with unicorns and one with the words of Taylor Swift's latest song. The others were boxed and disposable. Music blared and she glanced at the two men trailing her. They must be a little hot by now, the left rear window being stuck in a position not fully closed but not completely open either. The sun crept higher in the sky just topping the long leaf pines that lined the interstate making it hard for her to see the path that was just ahead of her. She drove, checking her speedometer every couple minutes to make sure she wasn't trying to rush things.

In the blink of an eye the two cars pulled onto the university campus, its old red brick and columns standing their ground. No one greeted them or guided them as they had when she had taken a tour. Today it was a Covid ghost town. But still, you would think that there would be a gentle flow of staff or faculty or at least a maintenance crew. In front of the dorm she was assigned stood a white tent, the kind that sprang up at national disaster sights. A lone woman sat several feet inside, barricaded by three rows of plastic buffet tables, a barrier reef. The imposed distance would save everyone's lives should a droplet of poison pass between them. Other than her, the landscape was barren. Like Marines entering a military zone, the trio suited up for the encounter. Mask first, then face shield, then courage. In unison, the three emerged from their vehicles and approached the tent, the girl hanging back and letting her father take the lead. That had become the choreography of their lives since her mother died; dad would dive into the water first to check the depth and make sure that no hidden dangers lurked, girl would follow feeling safe, stepfather would stand on the shore and cheer, keeping an eye out for invaders. Well-rehearsed, they no longer needed to even glance in each other's direction to confirm that the maneuver was mutually agreeable.

Once check-in was complete, out came the pillows, sheets, posters and electronics, all delivered to the service elevator where, as instructed, only father and daughter proceeded to drop everything in the room. Exactly one trip later they were finished. Room number 12 welcomed them with two twin beds, two desks, two closets, two chairs and one frightened looking roommate who sat stiffly on her bed. Her parents had already departed, heading home as soon as the unloading was complete. Not a sound reverberated from the hall or the campus beyond the window. Shadows from the mountainous pines outside danced on the unmade bed. The girl's father hugged her and exited. She hung her head out the window and blew a kiss to her stepfather who waved from below. Was he smiling? No way to know these days. She turned to the roommate and smiled at her, but of course, the roommate had no idea. It was Monday. Classes were scheduled to begin on the following Monday. For the next five days the two girls sat in the dorm room which had assumed the aura of a prison cell, leaving only for meals consumed outside at tables scattered safely apart from the pitiful spattering of fellow students who looked sheepishly at their fellow diners pecking at their paper plates. The inaugural pre-autumn sounds of academia—marching bands practicing, traffic grumbling, sopranos warming their vocal cords from upper windows—were all conspicuously absent. The atmosphere was what one would expect from outer space: deathly quiet, solitary, and ominous. No sign of life, just a pesky sense of fear for no named reason.

As the days passed, text messages flew in a triangle from daughter to father to stepdad.

"How are you doing?"

"Ok, I guess."

"Are you meeting people?"

"Not really. We aren't supposed to socialize."

"You ok?"

"There's nothing to do. Classes don't start for days."

"Made any friends yet? Transition to college is always hard, even without the virus."

"I want to come home. This is awful."

"Ok with me."

"Me too. Come on home."

Before the sun descended on day five, she bid her sullen roommate farewell. It had been nice to meet her, she wished her the best, she hoped she didn't screw things up for her. Sullen Roommate was already envisioning her own car packed to the gills with towels, electronics, clothes, shoes, and the very bed linens she was currently residing in. In the exact reverse order that she had loaded her car to move to college, the daughter repacked the cargo area, then the back seat, then the front passenger seat. She again summoned Aaron and Alexander and let them serenade her back into the swamp from whence she came.

Pulling into her father's driveway, she immediately spotted her stepfather's car parked just behind her dad's. Odd, for it wasn't even Tuesday. The two men were awkwardly perched in opposite rockers on the front porch, beers in hand. A fan stirred the August humidity that shrouded them. They came to life when they saw her car nosing towards them, headlights strobing their existence. She stepped out of the car and stood motionless except for the tears that were puddling in her eyes. Her father rose and wordlessly moved down the front steps towards her, arms unfolding into an invitation. He wrapped them around her, and she closed her eyes, forcing the tears on a ride down her cheeks.

"It's ok."

"I'm sorry. I'm so sorry. I just couldn't do it."

"It's ok, honey. Not your fault."

From the porch the stepfather bellowed.

"It's this damned virus! It's not you! Damn! I'm glad you're back!"

"I'm always glad you're back," confessed the father, a melody to her ears.

They hugged tighter as the secondary voice harmonized from the porch.

"Hey! Your dad cooked pork roast and I'll share it with you if you're hungry."

Her sniffles evolved into a tender laugh.

"I'll eat. I'm sick of that awful cafeteria take out garbage. I'm hungry."

"Good! Let's eat! That man on the porch can unpack your car after dinner." They all laughed, as dad further took the reins.

"Let's eat. I'm hungry. We're all hungry!" And indeed, they all were.

Jim Bellar

Mama, I Need Some Money!

The chipped, concrete porch steps to Mama's home were like an old friend to Tommy. He had climbed them thousands of times as a child and as a man. When he was seven years old, he broke off a tooth on the fifth step, and thirteen years later, he got married on the top step with family and friends looking on from the shady, front yard.

Mama's house was much like her—strong, simple, resilient.

Her father ran bootleg whiskey from a small, sliding window on the back porch. One night she saw him slit a man's throat for trying to steal money from him. Her husband, Larry Joe, died a long, slow death in the back bedroom from smoking three packs of Pall Malls a day.

Loaning money to people who couldn't borrow from the bank was Mama's main source of income. Interest rates were high and she kept a ledger of the date they borrowed, how much and when they would pay it back. She had no tolerance for excuses.

"I got one rule," she would say holding up her index finger, "you better pay Mama on time!" They did.

Tommy was Mama's only child, and he made at least one reference to her in every conversation he had.

"Yeah, Mama said it was going to be a bad winter this time," Tommy told his neighbor who asked how much firewood he should cut. "Mama said only people that are up to no good are out after seven at night," he recited to a friend who wanted him to go to a high school basketball game in a neighboring town.

And Mama had special senses. She knew when something was wrong, could smell a bad deal or when somebody was lying. Tommy always told the truth.

"Mama, Mama, you in there?" he said peering inside the screen door from the front porch.

"Yeah, that you, Tommy?" she yelled in a gravelly voice.

"It's me."

"Well come on in here, son."

Tommy entered the hallway and plopped down on the brown,

Naugahyde sofa in front of the living room fireplace. Pictures of him in every stage of development lined the walls and filled rows of shelves on the bookcase.

Mama raised him right—he went to church, didn't gamble, drink, or even curse. But after all that clean living, he was there today to ask Mama to help save his marriage, his kids, and the respectable job she got him down at the courthouse.

"You want some sweet tea?" Mama's green bonnet covered a grey, braided, waist-length ponytail. A simple print dress fell to her mid-calf and ended above tan, earthy work boots.

"Yeah, that'd be mighty fine."

"I'll have to make some; I'll be back in a minute."

He remembered the day she appeared in his office—her smile, those tight-fitting clothes and intoxicating fragrance, the way she talked. He'd never heard anything like it. His heart raced; he could barely keep his balance.

"Hello, I'm Miette," she said extending her hand. "Are you the person in charge?"

He trembled when he felt the soft flesh of her hand. "Yes ma'am, my name's Tommy Swindle."

"Well Tommy," she smiled, "I need to get a license plate for our car. We just moved to town."

He could have stopped it right there, kept it strictly business, but he couldn't help it. He'd never seen a woman that exuded such passion and confidence.

A few days later, he saw her strolling around the town square with her husband.

"Well, hello, Tommy. It's so good to see you again," said Miette softly shaking his hand. "This is my husband, Pierre; the principal at Crib's Creek. Tommy has an important job at the courthouse."

"Miette told me about your eagerness to help her the other day," Pierre said as he shook Tommy's hand. "It's refreshing to meet someone who works for the government that's not an idiot," Pierre smiled.

"Aw, I'm just an ol' country boy trying to live by the word of the Lord."

"Well that sounds like an ambiguous goal, but I wish you the best."

She attended Tommy's church the following week where she turned every man's head in the congregation. Her well-toned legs flexed under the pressure of ruby red stiletto heels; her derriere swung between the aisles like a pendulum on an expensive clock as she made her way to the front pew.

Miette called his office the following Monday to see if he would come by their house on the way home. She wasn't sure their license plate was installed correctly, and she needed the help of a "professional."

He had never made a house call about license plates, but found himself eager to fulfill her request later that afternoon. "Yeah, that's how it supposed to look," he said rising from a kneeling position in her gravel driveway.

"Well, thanks so much for your trouble. I insist that you come inside for some lemonade. That's the least I can do," said Miette.

"I really need to get going. I told my wife I would take her and the kids to the softball game."

"Please, it will just take a minute," she insisted. "Pierre had to work late, so why don't you have a seat in the living room and I'll bring you a drink."

Miette delivered the glass of lemonade to Tommy and dripped part of it on the crotch area of his plaid, polyester slacks.

"Oh Tommy. I'm so sorry. I'm so embarrassed."

She wiped his wet pants firmly with a dishcloth in a circular motion. He soon became aroused and uttered some words of weak resistance. "Mie-ette, what you—I can't—uh—I can't."

"Does that feel good?" Miette purred as she unzipped his pants.

"Lordy, yes," was all Tommy could utter as he pointed his nose at the ceiling and scrunched his eyelids tight in their sockets.

"This is just an hors d'oeuvre," she whispered. "We'll find another time for the main course at the Pawnee Motel."

"Lordy, yes, yes," was all Tommy could say.

"Here's your sweet tea," said Mama. "What you want this afternoon?"

The phone rang in the kitchen.

"Hold on." Mama picked up the phone and began talking to someone about mowing the hay on one of her three properties in the county. She quizzed the caller about the price, how much time it would take to mow it and calculated the cost per acre in her head.

Tommy wondered how he would start the conversation when she returned. Guilt and embarrassment consumed him. Why did he have to have sex with her? Couldn't he have been stronger? The sin had manifested itself in a piece of paper hidden deep in his jacket pocket.

To: Tommy Swindle

For: Services rendered

Amount: $1,200

Payable: August 4, 1963

Note: There is physical proof of this transaction. This matter needs to be taken care of immediately.

Tommy was not poor, but he didn't have that kind of money. On his salary, he could pay the mortgage and the basics but there was nothing left at the end of the month. He thought of things he could sell and people who might loan him money. One night he even got down on his knees in the dark living room and asked the Lord for help. He never heard back and that's why he was sitting on Mama's couch in the middle of the afternoon on a weekday.

Pierre delivered the invoice on a Friday afternoon after Tommy's co-workers had left for the day.

"Tommy, I would like a few moments with you to discuss some business."

"Business?" he said with a puzzled face.

"I'm afraid we have a situation," Pierre said.

"What kind of situation?" Tommy echoed, growing more concerned.

"I only met you once and I can't even remember your name."

"It seems like you recently had sex with my wife," Pierre said in a matter of fact voice. "That would probably not be considered as living by the word of the Lord and it would not serve you well if it was known in this little town."

"I don't... know.... what you're talking about." Tommy stuttered. "What do you mean?"

"Surely you've seen farm animals do this. Miette spilled lemonade on your pants and you met her later at the Pawnee Motel where you had your way with her. Would that be accurate?"

"I-I-I don't know."

Pierre placed a recorder on the counter and pressed the "play" button. "Maybe this will help you remember."

"Oh Tommy, you're such a big boy, you make me feel so good," a woman cooed through the speaker.

Pierre stopped the tape.

"Whoa there Tommy, it sounds like you did an exceptional job. You should be very proud."

Pierre laid pictures on the counter of Tommy and Miette in bed. He threatened to send them to courthouse workers and give his wife a copy of the recording. Tommy's life would be ruined— his job, church, family—everything would be gone, because of one stupid mistake.

Why did he think he could get away with this? The Bible says "do not lead us into temptation." Why didn't he listen? This had to be the work of Satan.

"All right, I'll think about it and let you know," said Mama hanging up the phone. "That was Narvis Pennington. He said he would cut the hay on the old Spring Hollow farm and the Petty Road place for thirty dollars. That's pretty good for 200 acres. Don't you think?"

"Well, I guess that's a pretty good deal. That's a lot of land," Tommy said taking a sip of sweet tea.

"Tommy, you got something on your mind. What is it?" Mama asked. He always felt she could look inside him and see his soul churning. It made him uncomfortable.

"I was just doing some thinking. Thinking about life and stuff and what it all means."

She sat her sweet tea on the glass top table and placed her bonnet on the back of the couch. "Now Tommy, you didn't come over here in the middle of the day to talk about life, did you? You've never asked me anything about that before. Is Wanda pregnant again?"

Tommy exhaled and then blurted out: "Mama, I need some money!" He tucked his head between his shoulders. "Lord, I need it now, I mean right now!" he said, violently shaking his head back and forth.

"What in the heavens has happened to you Tommy Lee Swindle?"

"I can't talk about it, Mama. I wish I could. I wish I knew what to do!"

"You're acting like a man who's lost his damn mind," she shouted.

"I'm sorry Mama. Something's happened and that's all I can tell you."

"How much money?" she barked.

"Twelve hundred dollars," said a sniffling Tommy.

Mama leaned forward on the couch. Her eyes glazed over while she tapped her fingers on the glass tabletop like she was operating an adding machine.

"Tommy, that's a lot of money, a lot of money. You're going to have to tell me what it's for. You're going to have to be a man. There's nothing you've done that can't be fixed. When people come here wanting to borrow money, it's just like the bank. I need to know where it's going and when it's coming back. I'm getting old and I can't die in the poor house. I can't do it."

"I've got myself into a situation and it's going to be bad if I can't come up with the money. It's going to be really bad."

"Tommy, you're a good Christian man, a family man, somebody with a good job, and a future. I've known all kinds of people in my life—liars, cheats, people who would do anything for a dollar. You're not like that. Your daddy tried to be a decent man, but the devil was on his shoulder most of his life. He couldn't help drinking, gambling, and chasing women. If he hadn't died when he did, I'da killed the son-of-a-bitch myself." She grabbed her glass and gulped the sweet tea until it was half gone. "I remember one night he came home so drunk he couldn't even tell me his name. He fell on the floor and I wrapped him up in a blanket and beat the ever-loving shit out of him with a poker iron. I never could get the blood out of that blanket and had to throw it away," said Mama shaking her head. "Aunt Mary gave me that blanket as a wedding present."

"Is that how Daddy got that broken arm?" asked Tommy in disbelief.

"Yep, I told everybody he got jumped at the beer joint, that sorry bastard. He wasn't good for nobody, even himself. Now you're not like your daddy, but you've got some of him in you. Which part is it?" she pried.

Sweat rolled down Tommy's face and arms; his white cotton dress shirt was soaked from the armpits to his belt line.

"Mama, I'm begging you. Please don't ask me what I done."

"Son, the only reason we have money today is that I took it away from your worthless daddy and made good decisions. I didn't take the easy way out and you're not going to either."

"Oh Jesus, Mama, Jesus!"

"Son, you're going to have to put your faith in the Lord and trust that everything is going to be alright."

"You sure Mama?"

Mama nodded her head.

"Whew—whew," Tommy exhaled.

"Now what happened?!" Mama demanded.

"You want to know what happened!?" Tommy screamed, jumping to his feet. He started toward the front door and walked back to the sofa. "A woman got me down, captured my manhood and then pulled me into her passion pit where I drove the devil's wagon straight through the gates of HELL!!! I couldn't stop! I lost control! I shouldn't have been there and now I have to pay the price! Jesus Mama! Why? Why? Why?!"

Tommy, sobbing, fell to the fetal position in the matching fake leather recliner while Mama sat stone-faced, looking straight ahead.

She cleared her throat and leaned back against the couch.

"Son, that's some expensive whoopee," she said in a matter of fact tone. "She wants you to pay her for that?"

"Her husband does," said Tommy.

"What do you mean her husband?"

"He took 'pichers' and has a recording of us going at it."

Mama put her hand to her mouth. "Hmmm. Tommy, something ain't right."

"They said if I don't pay them, they'll send the 'pichers' to everybody in the courthouse. They mean business, Mama. Wanda will leave me and I'll lose my job and my family and the church won't let me in and …."

"STOP! Tommy, you've got to get a hold of your damn self." Mama leaned forward. "Now I'm going to be honest with you. If you weren't my only son, I'd kill you for being so damn stupid. I know you're just a man and that's what men do, but what you don't understand is—there's always a price to pay. Now, I'm going to give you that money, but know that you may still be found out. You're probably not the only one they've done this to and word gets around fast in this little town."

"Mama, I feel like a fool."

"Hush now." She straightened his shoulders with her hands. "Don't say a word to anybody and come by the house on Friday at lunch. It's going to take a while to get that much money together."

"Okay Mama," he exhaled. "Okay."

"Tommy, I want you to know that Mama may not be able to fix it this time. These are not good people you're dealing with," she said as she picked up the tarnished poker iron from the fireplace and raised it behind her head, "and we'll have to do what we'll have to do!"

Lori Ann Stephens

Let No One Fear Me

The first time it happened, Sarah wasn't worried. She'd been startled, but who wouldn't be a little frightened to be wakened in the middle of the night, the crown of your head yanked up by someone's fist? She'd screamed out of surprise more than pain. Her husband Jack was a vivid dreamer and had taken to startling them both awake in sudden jerks or spontaneous song. Only the week before, he'd risen from bed belting out Otello's "Niun mi tema," which set the neighbor's dog into a frenzy.

At Sarah's yelp, he'd let go and bolted upright.

"What?" Jack murmured with the muddy voice of sleep. They both sat stunned, Sarah rubbing her scalp and moaning "Ow," and Jack falling back onto one elbow and blinking before asking again, "What's wrong?"

"You pulled my hair," Sarah whispered. She hoped they hadn't awakened Lanie, their teenaged daughter.

Jack patted her head and pulled her body into his. "I'm sorry." He nuzzled his face into her hair, inhaling her. "I was dreaming we were in a ship. And you'd fallen over the side. And I was trying to save you."

He pieced it together, the gravel of sleep still in his throat and eyes. When he was younger, he could never recall his dreams and wondered, in fact, if he was capable of dreaming. But lately, he'd jolt himself awake, the echo of his own gasp still in his ears, and have the uncanny feeling of having just walked into a web. He'd look around the blue-lit room slightly embarrassed, as though the furniture was judging him.

He blinked again, and his clouded eyes cleared. "Are you okay?"

She grunted and rolled toward him. "Yes."

He leaned back and opened his right arm to her. She nestled her head on his shoulder and shuffled until her ear didn't hurt and her hair wasn't pinched and she could smell his buttery exhalations and could fall back to sleep in this crook, her favorite place.

A ship, she'd thought as she drifted back to sleep.

So real, he'd thought, and drifted, too.

The next morning, they'd talked about it over tea. He'd recounted his racing heart as her body dangled over the ocean and her hands gripped to his arm, and she laughed and told him he'd better grab her wrist next time because her hair was falling out by the clump-ful lately.

"Could be hormones," she mumbled to herself and twirled a graying curl with a finger.

"Wrist. Duly noted," he said, and kissed her on the crown of her head. "I really feel bad about it."

A week later, Sarah and Jack laughed as they told their friends Carina and Joe about the terrible dream over dinner.

"He was saving me from drowning," Sarah said, and finished off her Merlot. "I was miffed for about five seconds. Until I saw his poor face. So sad and confused. My poor Jack." She cupped his jaw in her palm and shook her head and laughed again.

"Well, I couldn't let her drown now, could I?" A trace of guilt was still etched in Jack's smile.

"See?" Carina held up her wine glass, "even when he's sleeping, he's a regular Prince Charming. We knew what we were doing, didn't we Joe?" Joe and Carina had introduced them at the fundraiser.

After dinner, the two couples kissed cheeks, said goodbyes, and knew they wouldn't speak to each other again for another month or two, maybe longer? Sarah and Jack loved their oldest friends, but they were quite happy to escape the expectations, the grudges, and other trappings of friendship that hung over the heads of younger couples. After Carina and Joe had arranged the first successful blind date, Sarah and Jack slowly peeled away from social events and gravitated together, hand in hand, toward the solitude of their own orbit. They preferred it that way.

But the second time it happened, there was no tittering laughter. No animated narrative to recount over braised salmon at Lavendou. Because he'd honestly hit her. Planted his elbow on her right cheekbone, hard enough to leave a welt, and that was something one couldn't spin into a civilized anecdote no matter how accidental or ironic. This time, her cry was swallowed by the pain. She flicked on the lamp and, stunned, cradled the red throb of her cheekbone.

Jack lugged himself onto his elbows, bleary-eyed. "Are you okay?"

"You elbowed me," she said. A confusing spiral of humiliation and anger rose up her spine.

"Oh. Did I?"

She held her cheek and waited for him to jump from the bed to retrieve an ice pack. He rubbed his eye and squinted. She waited for him, could see on his face, the reaches and pulls as he climbed the rope to consciousness, knot over knot, up to Sarah.

"I think I was dreaming of a burglar. I was fighting him. I'm so sorry." He pulled her arm toward him and tried to tuck her into the crook of his shoulder, but it was no good. Her cheek was still throbbing, and when she closed her eyes, Sarah realized that she'd somehow, impossibly, *seen* his elbow at the moment of impact, which made her cheek ache even more.

She pulled away, irritated that he could not control his limbs, and stumbled to the kitchen for an ice pack. When she returned to bed, Jack stirred again, wrapped his arm around her waist, and pulled the weight of her against him.

"Are you okay?" he asked in a sleep-drunk stupor.

"Yes. But that's going to leave a mark." Sarah's eyelashes fluttered under the bite of the ice pack.

"I'm sorry, baby. Stupid burglar," he mumbled.

"Just. Maybe…" She extricated her torso from his embrace and turned away to click off the lamp. She stayed there on the edge of the bed with the ice pack balanced on her cheek.

After a minute, the space between them was oddly unbearable, so her toes found his feet, and within a few seconds, their legs were intertwined like summer vines. But sleep wouldn't come easily for either one. Jack kept shooing away visions of his burglar. And Sarah kept imagining her hair knitted in Jack's fingers, her scalp peeled away from her skull, her own face the stricken visage of Holofernes.

The next morning, Sarah stared at her reflection in the mirror, half-relieved to find no bruise from Jack's elbow, but oddly half-hurt that there was no the evidence of the attack. As though she had dreamed it. It wasn't really an attack, though, was it?

No. Jack would have crumpled at the word. He could hardly let himself think of what he'd done. He wasn't his father. It horrified him to think that he could hurt Sarah. His darling girl. It made his hands tremble.

And so, trembling, Jack brought Sarah her tea as she sat at the vanity and applied her moisturizers. He winked at her reflection and kissed her ear.

"Good morning, baby."

"Morning, prince."

She went to work at the museum, ate lunch in the cafeteria with Linda and Genevieve, met with the committee about the Art-mobile grant for the children's program. Every once in a while, her fingers brushed her cheek to find that yes, the bone was still sore. Yes, it had really happened. Her darling Jack had walloped her in his sleep.

Oh, Jack.

He was a knight to lost geckos and wayward spiders. Re-homed them via paper contraptions to the rose garden. He was so principled, he could barely reconcile the idea of a wedding ring and his solemn oath to respect her autonomy. But not everyone knew him like she did, and if she'd asked Linda or Genevieve at lunch, "Have your husbands ever hit you in their sleep?" who knows what horrors they'd privately harbor about Jack?

It's age, she finally decided. Something happened when he turned fifty, as though someone had flipped a switch that allowed him to speak in dream-tongues and trapped his puppet-limbs in an endless spinning wheel.

Sarah touched her cheek again as she drove home, and something bubbled up inside her. She was surprised to find herself smiling and shaking her head. Poor Jack. He was probably dying of shame. He'd kissed her excessively that morning, each kiss an apology.

Lanie was used to her parents' affections. When she was little and saw them kiss, she'd run over and wedge her little body between them, crying "No no! My Daddy!" Even then, Lanie knew that her parents' love for each other was something so sacred it was the one thing she had no power over. She couldn't play her parents to get her way because the other parent was always right. Besides, they were too busy flirting with each other. At six, it was unsettling. At eleven, it was embarrassing. Now, at sixteen, she'd found peace with it. At least it was better than her friends' parents, who were divorced or separated, or worse: incorrigibly together.

"Can you see a bruise?" Sarah asked Lanie in the garage.

Lanie hardly glanced over before tossing her backpack in the back seat. "No, why?"

"Nothing. Just...I bumped it yesterday." She didn't know why she lied. It was Lanie, for goodness sake. Lanie of all people knew her tender Jack.

"Can I drive?" Lanie asked. "I need the hours."

"Sure," Sarah sighed, unbuckled her belt, and walked around to the passenger side.

Lanie adjusted the mirrors and driver's seat while her mother pulled the driving log from the glove compartment.

"Lanie, did you hear anything from our room night before last? Like a little muffled scream? Or a few nights before that?"

Lanie glowered at her mother. "Uh, gross. No, Mom."

"Oh, Jesus. Grow up. I wasn't talking about *that*."

"Shhh. Teenager driving. I need all my faculties."

"Yeah, and I need a glass of wine. The way you drive."

Lanie bore Sarah's teasing in stride. Anything was better than driving with her Dad, who white-knuckled the Oh-Jesus handle and shouted, "Watch out!" at every intersection.

No one's honest about the way your body turns against you as you age. How you lose control. Sarah thought about this as she watched an elderly couple stand in front of the Modigliani. The old man shuffled to a bench, but the woman took a step toward the painting and leaned in as though she were about to initiate a private conversation with the Lady on the canvas.

Sarah fought the urge to sidle up to the old woman and ask too-personal questions. Does he talk in his sleep? Do his arms and legs flinch like a hound dog napping in the sun? Because that's what Jack had started doing a year or so earlier in his sleep. Little incomprehensible conversations at midnight. Feet twitching and arms composing, often ending with a flinch so strong, it jolted him awake. It wasn't until after the elbow incident, when Sarah started having trouble falling asleep, that she realized maybe *this* was why old couples began sleeping in separate beds. Not because of snoring, but because of fear. Tell me you still sleep together, Sarah wanted to ask the old woman. Tell me, what's going to happen to us in ten years?

The doctor called it a corneal abrasion.

"Is that bad?" Sarah asked her.

"It's bad enough that you came here. But it doesn't look too bad. It's a scratch with a scary name. What happened again?"

Sarah looked at her ridged nail beds. For three months, Sarah and

Jack had slept without incident. But just when Sarah began to fall asleep easily, she was awakened by Jack's groan and lurching arms. Her eyes flew open and she drew back her head, but not before Jack's fingernail caught the edge of her cornea. She'd caved into a ball and immediately began to cry, not just because of the sudden pain, but because of the betrayal of it all. Because of the cruelty of the world. Because she couldn't feel safe with the tender man who loved her more than anyone in the world. Because in dreams, their brains had turned against them without permission or conscience.

"Oh no," Jack had said again. And again, he'd pulled her thick waist toward him and tried to give her solace. And again, she'd dragged herself to the freezer for the cold pack, stumbled half-blind back to bed, and perched the poultice atop her eyes as she lay there, failing to fall back to sleep.

"What happened?" Sarah answered the doctor. "My husband talks in his sleep, and he sometimes jolts around." She waved her hands in the air, a poor attempt that looked more like a disco dancer than a night terror.

"Ah," the doctor nodded vaguely and said something about eye ointment and avoiding bright lights. Sarah waited, but the doctor didn't probe about her domestic situation. She didn't ask if Sarah felt fear at home. Wasn't that what doctors were supposed to say: are you afraid in your own home?

In fact, Sarah had already planned a response: *We're fine. We just need a sleeping pill that will stop all of his…activity.* But the doctor handed Sarah a prescription for the corneal abrasion, and nothing more was said about it. As though this is what happens in the sunset of your fifties.

For the next two days, Sarah walked around with grit in her eyes. Every blink was an insult. She placed the antibiotic on her bedside table. She wasn't angry at Jack. She was angry that every night now, she lined up a row of pillows between them and clung to the edge of the bed, just in case. Sulky that Jack had withdrawn, turtle-like in his shyness, as though he were afraid of *her.* She grieved the loss of Jack's shoulder and his toothpaste-breath as he fell asleep with the bridge of his nose against her forehead. She clung to the bed sheets, unmoored, her blood coursing as she rocked herself to sleep.

"Good night, baby," he said and reached over to pat her hip, but his hand landed on the pillow embankment instead.

In the lamp light, Jack read about paleontologist digs and the new *nanotyrannus* and mysteries that never ceased to be unearthed. Something deep within him trembled, awed at these millennial layers, these mortals, eroded and denuded by weather and time. And when he finally clicked off the lamp and pulled the covers to his chin, he whispered again, "Night, baby," and wrestled with the edge of consciousness.

He woke in a paroxysm. There she was in a stranglehold, his wife at the end of his hands. It was a like a horror movie, the frame of Sarah's face frozen before him, her shocked eyes pleading with him, his eardrums pounding. The horror of it jolted them both awake. He shot up, drenched in sweat, and looked over at Sarah, who was propped on her elbow and twisted bleary-eyed at him.

"Jack?" she asked, rubbing her eyes.

He sighed and nodded and breathed and breathed until his heart rate slowed. She lay back down, and he held his forehead and swallowed a cry.

Why would he dream such a horrible thing? He lay back again and studied Sarah's profile in the dark. He wanted to touch the edge of her hip, but his hand was still trembling. He restored the pillow barrier between them and turned toward wall. Shame spread across him like a fever.

Was he alone here in this undertow? Was he a monster? Sleep was the only place that could untether him, the only unmooring that love couldn't fasten. As he fell into his dark dreams, Jack searched for her, her toes, her ankles, aching with tenderness, and crushed by things he could not control and that she could not utter.

Grant Deam

White Rock Quarry

I used to think I was entitled to almost everything, even helping people. That's why I offered him a ride, this kid dressed in all black walking along the shoulder of West Main. I was on my way home from golf practice and didn't recognize him. Didn't realize he was Mike Bowers's little brother, Will.

Mike was two classes ahead of me at Belleriver High School and had gone to work for my father after graduating. I was a senior and planned on doing the same come summer. We would have been coworkers, but around a year after starting with the company, he quit. A cousin of mine was offered a journeyman position right before Mike completed his HVAC apprenticeship. Mike left town, and last I'd heard was living out by Central Canyons State Park.

I eased my dad's old DeVille to the side of the road. "Where you headed, partner?" I assumed he lived in one of the subdivisions dotting the outskirts of Belleriver, like me. It was hot for October, and he carried this sagging backpack weighed down by something heavy. A car passed as I rolled alongside him. "Hey, kid. I'm talking to you."

He stopped and took this deep breath, like I was wasting his time. "What do you want?"

"I'm just trying to help. I can give you a ride wherever you're going." I patted the passenger seat. "Come on. Hop in."

"My parents told me not to get in cars with strangers." He started walking again, bits of tire and broken glass along the shoulder ahead.

I inched forward. "I'm no stranger. I'm Eric Callahan. You probably know my dad, Big Tom?" Most people in town know my father. He's one of those loud types, has this big booming voice that's easy to pick out in a restaurant or at the high school football game. He likes to talk to everybody, and most people like to talk to him. "We've always lived here."

He stopped and took off his black sunglasses, looking at me for the first time. Maybe I should have realized then who he was. He had the same hazel eyes as his older brother, same reddish-brown hair, too. "Can you take me to White Rock Quarry?" His voice was flat, like he didn't really care if I could.

Like many people around here, I have a history with the quarry just outside of town. The mine stopped operating in the early 80s, but before closing, it employed generations from the area, including my grandfather. It's where he first learned about plumbing. He hauled ore and cut limestone for thirty years before starting the company my dad now runs.

"That's no problem. It's on the way." I put the car in park and reached over to unlock the passenger door. As he sat down, he was careful not to knock the bag into anything. He put it on the floor, shielding it between his legs. I put the car in drive. "What's your name, little man?"

"James Richardson."

"Oh sure! Your dad's the lawyer." He nodded, and we took off. The setting sun blazed through the windshield as we traveled west. "You know, I spent a lot of time out at the quarry when I was your age."

He didn't respond right away. "Doing what?"

"Fishing. Exploring. Getting into a little trouble." I winked, but he was staring out the window. "We'd save up our allowances until we had enough to buy some bait and snacks from that Shell station we just passed. White Rock was a little different back then. The water was so shallow, it was actually warm." I looked at the dark blue JanSport between his legs. Maybe there was a pair of swim trunks inside. "People get hurt out there all the time now. You aren't planning to go in, right? You could get hypothermia if you swim in the wrong spots. Do you know what that is?"

He faced me. "Do you think I'm stupid or something? Of course, I know what hypothermia is." I was starting to think the kid had something against me, which I couldn't stand. I wanted everyone to like me. I thought they should, and if they didn't, it was just a matter of time before they would.

Dust kicked up from the tires as I turned onto a gravel road. Fields of green soy waved in the light breeze. The corn had already been harvested, leaving certain plots barren. "Well, you don't have a pole." My golf clubs were rattling around in the trunk, so I had to raise my voice. "And you're too smart to go swimming. So, what are you planning to do?"

He gripped the handle of the JanSport. "Meeting some friends."

We came to a T, and I turned left back onto asphalt. "I hear all the high schoolers just come out here and drink now."

It was more of an underclassmen hangout—cases of warm Busch Light, handles of Smirnoff stashed in the woods, covered with leaves and branches. "Some do, and they're trespassing." I looked at the bookbag again. Were there a couple fifths inside? It would be dark in half an hour if that's what he and his friends were waiting for. "Drinking makes people stupid, though. A friend of mine lost a finger shooting off fireworks."

The speed limit went from 55 to 45 to 35 mph as we drove through the forest preserve. Sugar maples lined both sides of the road, their orange leaves made brighter by the sunlight. Maybe if I could get the kid to think about his family, he wouldn't make a bad choice. "You know my grandfather worked at the mine for thirty years."

"All your relatives work for your dad now, though, don't they."

It wasn't a question, and I didn't appreciate the tone. Was he criticizing my dad's business and how he ran it? Sure, it was inherited, but my old man busted his ass to grow it. "It's getting to be that way. Have to look out for your own people though, right?"

He didn't respond. We reached the end of the preserve, and the trees vanished, replaced by a steep drop-off. Then, we were gliding across the dryland dike cutting through the center of the quarry. The depth and size of the mine brought on a moment of silence. The layers and levels of the rockface, the old ramps snaking up the sides. We were witnessing generations of work, years of drilling, blasting, and hauling ore. Up this high, I couldn't see the bottom but imagined the icy water lapping hundreds of feet below.

"They mined limestone here. Most of the buildings on Main Street were built with rock from this quarry."

"I know. My mom works at the bank." He shifted in his seat, and whatever was in the bag clanked against the center console. I remembered that the Richardson kid's mom ran a dance studio in town. He was lying about who he was.

On the other side of the dike was the old employee parking lot for the Belleriver Stone Company. I'd try and level with the kid once we reached it. Whatever he planned to do out here—swim, drink, hide or retrieve something—it didn't matter. I'd been his age once. We all have. I needed to show him that I understood what he was going through *and* wanted what was best for him. That I was the rare high school senior who was both cool and responsible. Worthy of emulation.

A quarter mile later, I parked the DeVille between two faded yellow lines and cut the engine. Forgotten piles of stone cast shadows all around. In front of us, the open pit. There wasn't a soul in sight. I had expected to see another car in the lot, maybe some bikes in the grass near the woods. Had he lied about meeting friends, too?

The air smelled faintly of rotten eggs, the result of mineral decay within the mine. The odor clashed with my desire to revere this place. I opened the small compartment next to the steering wheel and removed a can of Skoal Peach. I began packing it, the snap of my index finger on the tin echoing off the rock. "You want one?" I placed a pinch under my lip.

"That stuff's gross."

I would have jumped at a high schooler offering me a chew at his age. Something felt off about this whole thing, like he had more control over the situation than me. "I guess you're right about that." I checked the rearview mirror and wiped away the loose strands of tobacco. He had moved the bag to his lap and was now clutching it against his chest. Was he going to bolt? It was just past 6:30 pm. I had quite a bit of freedom, but my folks still expected me home for dinner unless I told them otherwise. "Look," I said, spitting into an empty Gatorade bottle, "I can't let you out of this car until you tell me why you came here."

He removed his glasses and watched the sun sink under the horizon on the other side of the quarry. Bursts of orange and red reflected off his eyes, turning them almost golden. "One day, I woke up early to go fishing. I had to lie to my parents about where I was going. They wouldn't have understood." He looked directly at the fading light. "I rode out and found the perfect spot. I fished all morning and afternoon with no luck, but I kept trying. Kept casting and casting. It got dark, and I was ready to give up, but I finally got a bite." I couldn't tell if this was a true story, but it didn't matter. I had to hear him out. "The fish was strong. Whenever it took off in a different direction, I'd stumble forward and almost fall into the cloudy water. I had to jam the end of his pole between stones and take breaks from reeling."

"Eventually, I got the creature into the shallows. A big, beautiful trout. It had this bright pink streak down its belly." I've never seen nor caught any trout at White Rock. Maybe he didn't care anymore about keeping up the lie. He'd gotten to where he needed to be. "It was too pretty to take home and eat. That's what my brother said anyway, so I released it." He'd slipped up again, and this time I put it together. The Richardson kid didn't have siblings, and the only person I knew whose mother worked at the bank was Mike Bowers.

I looked out the window. In the sideview, fireflies glowed on the edge of the forest behind us. "That's a nice story." I knew things weren't going well for the Bowers. Mike had moved away, his dad was hardly working, and his mom wanted a divorce. Rumor had it there'd been an affair.

Had the kid come out here to do something horrific? More than a few people had died at the quarry. Most were accidents, but both teens and adults had come to this used up place to put an end to some unconquerable pain. A chill ran through me. "I need to ask you what's in the bag."

His right arm inched toward the handle. In one quick movement, he unlocked the door, shoved it open, and took off into the twilight, heading for the old entrance ramp. I followed, feet crunching over rock. The hum of the cicadas faded as I pursued him down, down, down. He couldn't outrun me, even in the flip flops I'd changed into after practice. I grabbed the backpack and pulled him toward me, hearing the clanking of metal again from inside. Glass bottles of liquor? A gun? "Kid, stop! I know who you are. I know your older brother." He kept twisting around, trying to break free. "Just hold on a second! Let's talk." We were sliding all over the gravel, the bag's material burning my palms.

He juked left, pivoted, and spun around, ripping an arm across his body. I lost my grip, but instead of sprinting further down the ramp, he ran back toward the parking lot. When I turned to follow, the rubber sandal slid out from under my foot. I heard a pop and knew I'd sprained an ankle. The pain was instant, causing me to go to ground. I'm not sure how long I sat there, but by the time I limped up to the parking lot, he was nowhere in sight.

My ankle throbbed. I could barely support my body weight and collapsed onto the driver's seat. The dome light revealed a lump the size of a golf ball. I felt sick and forgot about potential suicides and underage drinking parties. My senior season was now in jeopardy and for what? The sun was nearly gone, the sky a dark blue. Seven o'clock came and went. I considered calling the cops or my folks but instead started telling myself the kid would be fine on his own. Hadn't he been walking by himself to begin with? If he had planned to stay the night out here, he had likely prepared for it. The clanking I heard was just a lantern, some flashlights.

Night settled in. I turned the car on, beams shining over the open pit. By now, he deserved whatever was coming to him. But I didn't leave.

I couldn't. At some point, my mom called, and I said I was over at my cousin Wyatt's house helping him study. He was a junior at the time and a stand-out athlete. I'd been helping him stay eligible.

My ankle was stiff and cold to the touch. The pain was still there but less intense. I needed to get home and ice it, keep it elevated. I turned the car off and stepped out. Using the door to balance, I called into the darkness. "Come back!" What if I heard a blast? The shot from a Glock out in the woods? Or, what if the clanking had been from bottles of booze, and he got drunk and fell into the mine? What would people think of me?

Now, the rotten egg smell was overbearing. I packed another dip, and my heart rate quickened. All my life, I had considered White Rock almost sacred. For the kid, though, it meant something different. Something painful. And for the first time, I feared this place. I got back in the car and flashed the headlights on and off. Again, I reminded myself that he had been alone when I first saw him. I spit out the chew and started biting my nails. Then, shortly after 8:00 pm, some rustling, twigs and leaves crunching close by. I turned the brights on. A figure was walking through the smattering of trees on the north end of the lot.

He had developed a limp to match mine. Once he reached the gravel, he started taking these short, choppy steps, and it took him a while to reach the car. When he opened the door, the interior lights revealed nicks and cuts on his face and hands. Nothing too deep. Nothing still bleeding. Relief washed over me like a wave. I forgot about the pain and was grateful I hadn't just played a role in some tragedy. "What the hell were you thinking?"

"You should have left after you brought me here."

"And let you do something stupid?"

"What do you mean stupid?"

"I don't know. Get drunk, fall, and hurt yourself. You're Mike Bowers' little brother, and I know he left town a while ago." It was hard for me to say it. "I thought you might've come here because you were upset about that."

"I'm too young to drink, and I'm not suicidal or something." He didn't balk at the word. I started the car and began to drive. He didn't need to tell me where he lived. When we reached Main, he said. "Your dad is the reason Mike is gone."

Relief and frustration gave way to shame. "Now hold on. You can't go blaming other people for a choice your brother made."

"Sure, I can." I didn't know what to say. The job had started off as an opportunity but morphed into a type of rut. A reminder of class and company politics. Something Mike couldn't see himself getting out of or progressing up through.

I pulled into the Bowers' driveway. All the lights in the house were on. I imagined his parents, livid inside, and I didn't envy what he was about to walk into. When he opened the passenger door to leave, I asked him, "What were you doing anyway? Where did you go?"

"I was making that place useful again."

"You scared the hell out of me."

He stepped out of the car. "I would've done what I did with or without you." I made sure he walked inside before leaving.

On my way to school the very next day, I took the same road by the quarry heading the opposite direction. When I passed over the dike, I saw a message on the rockface. No one driving into town this way could miss it.

Up high on the stone cliffs, the words *COME HOME MI* were spray painted in black. The letters were thick at the top and thin toward the bottom. The first few were a dark, almost shiny black, but he'd ran out before he could complete the name. I have no idea how he got in position to tag the rock. He would have needed to repel from the top. A fall from that height would have killed him.

For months, I took roundabout backroads to avoid the quarry. I couldn't bear the sight of it. What he was willing to risk, all that pain. Over the years, some of the black has faded away due to rainfall, the passing of the seasons. But you can still make out most of it. I'm not sure if Mike ever saw the message. He did return, though, and I can't say I had anything to do with it.

Jen McConnell

The Irrational Constant

"You have a fever." Mom loved to point out the obvious. She took her hand from my forehead and picked up her coffee cup. "You should stay home from school."

"I feel fine," I lied.

"You stay up too late with those numbers. I don't know why—"

"Because it's important to me." I stood up and shouldered my backpack. If I could memorize almost one hundred digits of pi, she could at least remember why I was doing it.

Mom grabbed my arm. "I know it's important. I just don't understand why."

I pulled away, not in the mood to explain it again. Mom's attention could only last a few minutes. Sure enough, when I looked back, her eyes were closed, her mind back to the list in her head.

The List of Never Enough, I called it. At the top was never-enough-money, just edging out never-enough-time. Even though Dad paid child support, Mom said it wasn't the same. Adding a two-bedroom apartment to our bills brought us down a tax bracket, Dad tried to explain. Later, I asked my brother, Greg, what that meant.

"It means, dipshit," he sneered, "that while we were lower middle class before, we're now upper poor."

I didn't mind not getting an allowance or patching my backpack with duct tape. I'd learned to ignore the teasing a long time ago. What I hated was that everything had changed. Mom worked two jobs and was never around. Every other weekend, we stayed with Dad. He exhausted us morning to night with hiking, mini-golf, movies, anything but just hanging out like we used to. I especially hated lying on the saggy bottom bunk, pinching myself to stay awake until Greg was asleep. More than once I'd woken up with a spider crawling on me.

"You should at least wear shorts so you aren't so hot," Mom said.

I ignored her and pulled the front door closed.

Jog-walking to school, I recited the numbers. "Three point four one five…nine two six five three…" Pi was a mathematical constant that had no end when written. At least, no one had found it yet. That's what I liked about it. "…five eight nine seven nine…" That the end—the final number—was out there somewhere. Mathematicians had been working at it for centuries, and even though it had been parsed out to trillions of digits, there was still no end in sight. For all that uncertainty, no matter what size circle you measured, the ratio of circumference to diameter was always, constantly, pi. I'd explained this many times to Mom. "…three two three eight four…"

I arrived sweaty and dizzy to first period, having only reached eighty-seven digits. Of course I had a fever but I couldn't miss school. Tomorrow was March 14, the day of the Pi Contest. After deducting spring break, Memorial Day and two teacher in-service days, there were only fifty-seven days until school was out.

I hadn't missed a day all year. This year, the prize for perfect attendance was a trip to Disneyland on the last day of school. Only the few perfect attendance students and two teachers would go, paid for by the school. I'd been there with my family a few times for special occasions—we lived only an hour away. The last time we went was for my thirteenth birthday, right before the divorce. Disneyland without my family, especially Greg, would be infinitely better. The bell rang as I walked into History and slid into my seat next to Trae.

"You ready?" Trae asked.

"Up to ninety. Hope to get up to ninety-five tonight. That should be enough. I heard Tommy Falgren got—"

"Got to ninety-two, I know." Trae sighed. "Look, Stef and I are going to the mall after school. She said you could come."

"I can't."

"A couple hours at the mall won't hurt." She scowled as Ms. Dennison called for our homework. "You have all night to study."

I shook my head and Trae turned away. She knew I didn't have money for shopping but never stopped inviting me.

In Math, I finished the in-class assignment quickly and flipped over the paper to write out pi. Mom said I got my love of numbers from her dad. Grandpa lived only a few streets away from school, still in the house where Gramma died, the same house where Mom grew up. She'd gone to my high school. Her initials were carved into a locker in the junior's hallway but she'd never been interested in seeing it again.

By the time the lunch bell rang, my head was pounding. I threw up in my mouth a little just looking at the turkey sandwich Mom made. She knew I hated mayonnaise but half the time forgot. I threw the bag away and walked to the library. I couldn't bear to sit in the hot sun and listen to Trae, Stef and the others gossip.

I waved to Mrs. Faiges and took a seat at an empty back table. Most days, rather than go home, I studied in the library after school. I stayed until Mrs. Faiges turned off the lights. She almost always offered me a ride home and could almost always hide the pity on her face.

I laid my head on the table and closed my eyes. When summer came, I'd have to hang out at the public library, which smelled like cooked cabbage. With Dad gone and mom at work all day, Greg used me as his personal servant, under not-very-vague threats of violence. I wished I could go to a math camp or bring myself to fail a class so I could be assigned summer school. Before the end-of-lunch bell rang, I stopped by the desk to tell Mrs. Faiges I wouldn't be staying after school.

"You look like you should go home now," she said.

"I know."

"Here." She scribbled on a piece of paper and handed it to me. "Go see the nurse."

In the nurse's office, she waved away the paper I offered. "Don't need that to know you should go home," she said.

"Could I just stay here for a little while? Maybe I'll feel better." I laid down on the cot.

"I'm going to call your mother."

"No." I reached out to her. The nurse hesitated, then took my hand. "I have perfect attendance."

"You're sick."

"Please."

She sighed and let go. "Let me ask the attendance office how many periods count as a school day."

I curled up on the cot as she turned off the light and closed the door. The hallway outside quieted as students disappeared into classrooms.

If today counted as attendance, maybe I'd walk over to Grandpa's instead of going home. I could nap on his couch and then study my numbers. He'd order us a pizza and drive me home just before bedtime. I would feel better tomorrow and beat Tommy Falgren by at least two numbers. If today counted, I'd still have perfect attendance and get to go to Disneyland. I'd escape my life, if only temporarily, for a day filled with countless combinations of fun.

Kate Kaplan

POTHOLES

One: Meet Cute

Traffic was pissy in West Hollywood, but in Beverly Hills, Sunset was wide and the lights synchronized for speedy travel. Nina barreled west, songs about the glories of beer blasting from the country music station. Then, past the curves and swoops of Little Holmby, past the faux Bel Air gates, she hit a massive pothole. Her little Honda rocked and shuddered. A tire went flat—she could feel it—and something in the suspension broke. She felt that, too.

The car still moved, which was good, because stopping on Sunset would have been an invitation to a rear end accident. Nina took the first right, parked near someone's gated driveway, and examined the damage. It was as bad as she'd expected. She herself wasn't physically hurt, but the bumping and jarring made her heart beat faster, and the probable cost of fixing the car had her on the verge of tears.

She sat on someone's low stone wall and tried to calm down. Her phone was charged. The Auto Club's number was in her contacts. The Auto Club would save her. It would only—only!—be a question of time and money.

She tapped her password into her phone and discovered that the Auto Club wouldn't save her any time soon. She had everything but a cell signal.

The street was residential, but not the kind of residential that meant kids and basketball hoops and visible front doors where she could ring a bell and ask whoever was home to make a call for her. Birds sang over the swoosh of traffic on Sunset. Stands of bamboo whispered in the breeze. Magnolias were in bloom, and the street was white and pink with their meaty, brown-edged petals. The houses were hidden behind gates and walls and hedges.

She could buzz the buzzer at each gate, but the street was hilly and steep, the gates far apart, and the houses quiet. It was entirely possible that no one would answer, or answer with anything other than a quick dismissal. She could try to wave down a car, but there wasn't much traffic, and even if there were cars, it was entirely possible that no one would stop. She was going to have to walk down to the UCLA campus, over a mile away. Too bad she was wearing impractical kitten-heeled sling-backs.

Maybe if she buzzed enough buzzers, tried to flag down enough cars, someone would call the police. Maybe that was the best thing that could happen. It made sense to Nina, that the best thing that could happen was that someone would try to punish her for her misfortune.

Then her knight in shining armor showed up, the armor being a boxy, pale blue convertible the approximate size of a toddler's toy, driven by a very large (tall, not particularly thin) man who probably couldn't have fit in the car if the car had a top. The car had a personalized license plate: GO4ITT.*

Whatever it's seemed like so far, the speeding, the shoes, the license plate, the beer songs, Nina is sixty-six years old, and the man in the snappy car is seventy. A species of romance is about to begin, but don't worry, they're not going to have sex.

The sex lives of old(er) people is a big *ugh* for lots of people even without the comical addition of the pharmaceuticals probably required to make things happen. Pot bellies, saggy post-C-section bellies, assorted surgical scars, droopy butts, slack skin! Both Nina and the man in the car—his name is Barry—felt that *ugh* when they were young. In some ways, they still feel it, and it puts a crimp in their inclination toward romance.

Another thing that limits their romance: this is a classic meet cute, practically a scene from a nineteen-forties type movie, such a classic meet cute that when the pale blue car turned up, Nina thought, "meet cute." Nothing wrong with a meet cute, at least in some genres. The problem is that Nina's already had one, and the experience taught her to mistrust the whole idea.

Her first meet cute was when she met her husband, Carter, at an independent bookstore. He was tall, not bad looking, reaching for a copy of *The Western Garden Book* at the same time she was. They'd bumped heads, painfully. "It's for my sister," Carter had said, with a nice crooked smile. "I got head bonked for your sister?" Nina asked, flirty. "She appreciates it," Carter answered, mock serious.

Nina yielded the book. The rest was history—or comedy, or tragedy, depending on what part of the Nina-and-Carter relationship you were talking about.

The pale blue car paused in the driveway. Barry used his remote to open the elaborate, curlicued metal gates, but he didn't drive through them. He'd never had a meet cute, and the cuteness of this meet charmed him. So did Nina. She was petite, curly-haired, slumped over a phone he knew would be giving her nothing. She looked appealingly lost. Even more appealingly, her first words weren't lost. He asked if he could help her. She looked him over and said, sarcastically, even aggressively, "Nice car."

He loved the contrast; a feisty—spitfire!—damsel in distress. "Belongs to my daughter. She's in Boston, studying some damn thing, and I hope she learns enough to regret the license plate. In the meantime, I might look ridiculous, but this baby—" he patted the driver's side door "—is fun to drive." (His daughter, Ariel, was studying material culture. She'd never regret the license plate. She already knew that it was stupid, but she loved and honored her dopey teenage self.)

Despite her wariness, Nina liked Barry's attitude and his looks—a pleasingly open face, the kind of close-cropped hair that acknowledges and accommodates incipient baldness, a nice blazer—cashmere, she'd come to discover, and soft to the touch.

He looked so content and relaxed, so clean-shaven and pink-cheeked, that she found herself thinking that he'd just come from a tryst. It wasn't a word she ever used, but it sounded old-fashioned and like afternoon sex on good sheets. That was what Barry looked like, to her. (He'd come from his podiatrist.) Pheromones and the ability to detect them fade with age, and it was a medical fact that Nina's estrogen levels were lower than they had been, but she could smell the masculinity in Barry.

She knew that she should be holding out her Auto Club card and asking, in a tone of voice that was formal and polite, with just a hint of desperation, if he'd mind making a call for her. "Guy walks into an auto parts store," she said instead.** "Says 'I'd like a set of wiper blades for my Yugo.' The auto parts store guy thinks for a minute, and then he says, 'Sounds like a fair trade.'"

She'd heard the joke on the radio, years earlier, and related to it. She'd always had economy cars and she knew better than to believe in the existence of a fair trade.

Barry laughed, not politely but in an actual reaction to the joke. "Lord, I remember the Yugo. You know this one? When is a car not a car?" He answered his question immediately, pursuant to joke protocol. "When it turns into a driveway."

Nina's turn to laugh. "A kid joke. I like kid jokes."

She liked all kinds of jokes. She tried to remember every good and not-bad one she heard, so she could tell them to herself, driving to work on difficult mornings—most mornings. That way, she could guarantee that her day would include something funny. Something she liked. She knew that the practice was pathetic, but she did it anyway.

Barry liked jokes, too. At his first wedding, someone had wished him and his first wife a house filled with laugher—may your house be filled with laughter, that kind of thing. Barry had heard an order—*your house should be*—instead of the good wish, and it was one he wanted to obey. He liked jokes because he'd never had a house filled with laughter, except that lately, he filled the first floor of his house with laughter by watching stand-up comedy specials on TV. Something fun in his life, he'd think, and didn't let himself know that it was a bit pathetic.

"Ok, this isn't a kid joke," Nina said, "but maybe it counts because my son told it to me. Pirate walks into a bar with a steering wheel hanging out of his pants, and he says—" She stopped, because she was telling it wrong. She was ruining the joke. Barry—he'd introduced himself by then—wouldn't laugh. He'd be embarrassed for her. He'd *pity* her. It was the terrible risk of telling a joke out loud.

But Barry was waiting, as yet un-pitying. Nina found her courage and started again. "No, he walks into the bar and the *bartender* says, 'I don't know if you know this, but you have a steering wheel hanging out of your pants.' And the pirate says, 'Argh, I know, it's driving me nuts.'"

Barry laughed. Nina felt the warm glow of successful joke-telling, but after a second, she felt a bit of cold panic, too. She'd escalated the whole encounter by telling a joke that had testicles in the punch line. Why had she done that?

Two stupid reasons. The first, she understood and acknowledged. She did it because she wanted to. (As previously noted, she could smell his masculinity. She liked the smell of masculinity.) The second, even stupider, she didn't see. Against all common sense but in accord with her social conditioning—shining armor was expensive—she trusted Barry not to harm her because he was so obviously rich.

"Should I call the Auto Club?" he asked. "Only, you might want to hang out for a while. Friday afternoon rush hour." He saw a shadow cross her face and worried that he'd ruined everything by suggesting that she enter his house. Which of course she couldn't do. It felt as though they knew each other—pheromones?—but they didn't. "We can wait out here."

We can wait. They both let that go. They both let it stand.

Older backs don't appreciate backless stone walls, and Nina's back already hurt. Barry liked the little car, but it was truly cramped, and he felt it in his knees. He drove up his driveway and drove back down with a bottle of wine and a bag of pretzels on the front passenger seat and two floral-cushioned wicker chairs—chairs that spoke of ease and covered porches—jammed in the back, legs up, cheerful. "Do you need to call anyone?" he asked, when the chairs were in the driveway and the wine poured and the bag opened. "Your husband?" Nina was wearing a wedding ring, a wide gold band, maybe too wide for her delicate finger. Nina didn't answer. Her throat was blocked. Not literally, there was no tumor or inflammation, but it was blocked nonetheless. It got that way every time someone asked about Carter. The silence went on for so long that it said what she didn't want to say.

"He's not expecting me at any particular time," was what she finally came up with. Carter would be busy making one of the model ships he kept saying he could sell for good money but never did, or writing a letter to the landlord complaining about the neighbors, or organizing his meds, or sleeping. He might be angry if she was late and didn't call, but then, he was often angry when she was prompt. "I was headed to the beach," she added. "Sometimes, you just need to see the ocean."

Barry nodded in the way people do when they want to communicate that they understand, even if they don't understand. "A penguin decides to go visit some old pals at Sea World," he said. "He's almost there when his car breaks down, so he pulls into the gas station across the street. Gas station guy says that it'll be an hour, so the penguin goes over to Sea World, sees his friends, gets himself some ice cream, a vanilla cone. And you know what messy eaters penguins are, the ice cream's all over his face. Finally, the hour's up, he goes back over to the gas station, and the gas station guy says, 'Looks like you blew a seal.' And the penguin's furious. 'Leave my personal life out of this! Just tell me what's wrong with my car!'"

He changed the punch line on the fly. The way he usually told the joke, the penguin said, "no, it's just ice cream." That was too graphic for the occasion. Even so, he held his breath until Nina laughed.

She knew that it wasn't a good idea to laugh at a male stranger's blow job joke, but the wine, the smell of jasmine from someone's yard, the overpoweringly lovely pink and white magnolias, the fact that she wasn't in any of the places—work, home—that she was supposed to be—was disinhibiting. That was the word the doctor had used when her mannered, reticent father started grabbing the butts and breasts of the aides at the nursing home. The conduct was appalling, but Nina had savored the word.

Not just the wine and the jasmine and so on. Barry was enjoying her company. That was intoxicating, too.

For a second, in her day-drunk haze, she saw Carter leaning back in the wicker chair next to her instead of Barry—Barry turned into Carter, like a car turns into a driveway. Not Carter the way he looked now— hunched and angry, frightened and small—but the way he looked in their wedding picture, on display in their living room.

When the haze cleared, Barry was still talking. "Just *think* about that joke," he was saying. "It has to have started with a mechanic who liked the pun—"

"—I bet every mechanic likes the pun—"

"—but that wasn't good enough for this guy, so he thought, who or what would do that with a seal?"

"A penguin, which of course has a reputation for messy eating, so by the time you get to the punch line you're thinking about those penguin documentaries—"

"—and in joke logic, of course the penguin can drive—"

"—and talk," Nina finished, then paused. "People can be wonderful sometimes."

"Amen to that." Barry raised his nearly-empty glass.

Nina's mother had insisted that it was important to choose a spouse who had your same values and who wanted to live the way you wanted to live, city or country, buy or rent, kids or no kids, new restaurant every time or same old. Nina had done her best, but Carter had changed, or lied, or more likely she'd been driven by pheromones and hadn't listened very well. Or even more likely, it was stupid advice. Happiness only existed in moments, so why not choose someone for his pink cheeks and his pleasure in a silly car or his appreciation for a mechanic who liked, but wasn't satisfied with, a pun?

(A neighbor, driving past in a large, dark, SUV, shook her head at the eccentricity: Barry, known to her because he'd once done business with her husband, lounging in his driveway with some woman, laughing his head off. She mentally took him off the invitation list for a pretty nice party she was planning—unless that deal with her husband was still pending, better check.)

(This neighbor wouldn't have stopped for Nina, if Nina had tried to wave her down. She correctly connected Nina to the wrecked Honda, and found her unappealingly needy, not appealingly lost. The neighbor had her child—sixteen years old and looking at his phone—in the backseat. She believed that she had to teach her child to be wary of strangers.)

Nina and Barry talked—just talked—until rush hour was over. When the tow truck arrived, Barry looked sad. Poor little rich boy? Not exactly, but it was true that he'd spend the evening alone, heat up a sausage pizza even though he was supposed to be limiting carbs and calories, find a TV comedy special to watch, and go to bed lonely.

By then, Barry knew that Nina had a mid-level job in the risk-management division of a department store chain. She didn't have to tell him that the job was both insecure and poorly paid. He was an investor. He knew what was happening in the retail sector. At one point in their conversation, he was gripped by an impulse to give her a chunk of money. He could tell that her job, the husband who didn't need to be called, her life, was wearing her down, wearing her out, and that she didn't deserve to be worn down and out.

Giving her money wasn't possible, though, and he couldn't be sure that he'd have done it if it was. He was quite rich, but he hadn't gotten that way by giving chunks of money to strangers.

"Thank you for a lovely afternoon," he said, as the tow truck driver did his thing with chains and hitches.

Nina very much wanted to go up the driveway and see the house, which was no doubt spacious and calm and cleaned regularly. She very much wanted to touch Barry's open face and tell him jokes and see his smile, which was warm and appreciative. All she had to do, she thought, was to say that she'd like to take him out some time, for coffee, for drinks, to say thank you. Nothing wrong with a thank you, even from a married woman.

However. She knew that if she went into the house, if she kept telling him jokes and enjoying his smile, the envy, the pain every time she left, might kill her. And she'd have to leave. She couldn't stick her children with the burden of caring for Carter.

("Why does Mom stay with him?" Nina's son would ask his sister. "*I* don't know," Nina's daughter would answer. "Marriage vows? Because

he'd die if she left, and she's not a murderer?" "Because they can't afford
two rents," her brother would suggest instead.)

Nina put her hand on Barry's arm for a moment, discovered that his
blazer was cashmere, and soft, thanked him and said good-bye.
There! Aren't you glad I kept my promise about sex? Nina and Barry are.
It had been too long since Nina had let anyone new—except doctors—
see her naked body, the aforementioned sags and scars, let alone the
bunions on her feet, the spider veins on her thighs, the odd red dots
on her chest and arms that the dermatologist could remove, for money
she didn't have. Barry didn't think about his body that way, but he did
think about his vigor (by which he meant his erection); what it had once
been, what it was. He wanted to sleep with her—that's why he'd been
disinhibited enough to tell the penguin joke—but he thought that he
might try and fail, and he wasn't sure he could bear that.

They never saw each other again, though of course they had memories.
Barry found his sweet and poignant, but sad, too, and he let them fade.
Nina built on hers and embellished them so that the encounter grew into
an alternative life, and a place of refuge. Surprisingly, the existence of this
alternative made it easier for her to deal with Carter. She never told him
where she'd been all those hours, and he never asked.

Or Two: Despair

Dusk. Nina was driving on Hollywood Boulevard, listening to something
gruesome—it involved drugs and edged weapons—on the all-news
radio station. She didn't see the pothole until it was too late. Her Honda
dipped and lurched, then made a terrible grinding noise. The car still
moved, though, and there was a Pep Boys on the next block—the sign,
unlike the pothole, was clearly visible. What luck! she thought, what
irony, to break your car in a pothole right near the Pep Boys, a place that
fixed cars broken in potholes.

She pulled into the lot, but store was dark. The Pep Boys was (were?)
closing.

"You can leave the car," the last, locking-up employee said. "Someone
look at it tomorrow. Open 11 am."

"My car will be ok overnight?" Nina knew that it was stupid question,
but she was nonetheless infuriated by the employee's response—an
uncaring shrug.

He was young, she figured no more than twenty-five, and by his accent Russian or Armenian or something, no doubt hoping for a better life in America and possibly finding it, with a responsible job at Pep Boys. However, for all the talk Nina'd heard about the way other cultures respected their elders, *cared* for their elders, he was climbing into the only other car in the lot, a newish black truck, heedless of her welfare. Not even a "you ok?" or the offer of a phone, or a warning about the neighborhood.

The Russian, or whatever, backed out of his spot at speed like the jerk he no doubt was, made a quick stop, engine running, to stretch a chain between the posts that flanked the driveway, and drove off. The chain was laughably minimal as far as security went, but Nina figured that no one would try to steal her car, which was old and broken. It might make a tempting target for vandals, but there was nothing she could do about that, because she too might make a tempting target for vandals. She might not be ok overnight, or in fact much longer, in a parking lot at the corner of Hollywood and El Centro on a Saturday night. The area had come up in the world, but not by much, and given how far down it was when the upturn started, it still had a long way to go.

(Omar, the Pep Boys employee, would never have left his truck in that parking lot overnight. He was Bosnian, twenty-six years old, and he felt some guilt about deserting the old lady. His baba for sure wouldn't have approved. On the other hand—Pep Boys was barely visible in his rearview by now—fuck her. Born in America, by her attitude—like he owed her help—and her accent, but so weak that she couldn't make such a fat, careless country work for her. That shitbag of a car told the story. What was he supposed to do, take her to his house for a slice of baklava? Offer her a ride? She'd probably think he wanted to rape her. As if he would, old lady like that. Let her husband, who'd given her that thick gold wedding ring—that was a lot of gold—take care of her. Omar himself was on his way to his second job, and he couldn't afford to be late.)

"Really?" Carter asked when Nina called. "You know I don't like to drive at night. I mean, if you hadn't insisted on going to that ridiculous so-called art gallery . . ." Nina had been at a low-rent side-street gallery, ok, yes, a *garage* gallery, to see a co-worker's partner's fabric sculpture. The sculpture had been awful, but no matter what Carter thought, she couldn't have known that for sure, in advance, and even if he was right and she could have, it was somewhere to go when the errands were done and Carter had taken over the living room with his folding work table and his model ships.

"You obviously have your phone," Carter said. "Use one of your apps." He always pretended not to know the names. "Call a cab."

Thirty dollars, Nina thought, for a driver who might or might not be a good driver, a thief, a rapist, a murderer. Thirty dollars so that she could spend half an hour in a car that might or might not be any safer than the corner of Hollywood and El Centro. Still, calling Carter had been a not-nice thing to do, because she already knew that Carter didn't like to drive at night. He didn't like to go anywhere at night, and he didn't much like to go anywhere in the daytime, either. He was frightened of the night. He was frightened, period, end of story.

She locked the Honda for additional minimal security and headed toward the marginally safer but definitely better lit doughnut store down the street. She wasn't going to meet a cab driver, an Uber driver, in the dark driveway of a dark, empty parking lot.

Outside the doughnut store, she tapped her too-simple password (1010) into her phone again. Now that she'd called, Carter would be waiting for her, as anxious as she was about cabs and apps and drivers—more, because anxiety was his default interface with the world. She knew that she should hurry, but the store smelled wonderful. It had to be a stupid move on their part, Nina thought, making doughnuts so late in the day, but she was transfixed.

(The store was making doughnuts to sell later that night, when drunken young people left the clubs. By then, the doughnuts would be old, but the customers wouldn't have the capacity to notice that or the store's deliberate inaccuracies in ringing up purchases, giving change, adding tips to credit card slips. Saturday night was huge for the doughnut store.)

Nina had her coffee and doughnuts at the two-person-sized counter, looking out over the dirty Boulevard. The stars on the sidewalk were faintly visible under the streetlights, the stars in the sky not visible at all.

It's too easy, the contrast between the now-little-known people who have stars on the eastern end of the Hollywood Walk of Fame—Karl Dane, Jim Davis—and the stars in the sky. Still, the eastern end of the Walk of Fame actually exists, as does, as of this writing, the Pep Boys. It would be impossible for someone sitting where Nina's sitting, someone of Nina's disposition and in Nina's situation, not to notice the sidewalk stars and the lack of actual stars, not to feel the futility of it all, and as though her life was sliding away, wasted.

It wasn't always so. Nina hadn't been the kind of person who married someone who didn't like to leave the house, if there was a kind of person like that.

They'd met cutely in a bookstore, had an ordinary courtship of drinks and dinners; flirting, then sex; beach hikes and classic movies; had a wedding like all the weddings they'd ever been to. At twenty-eight, it was exactly what Nina wanted. Forty years later, she couldn't believe how meek she'd been when she was young enough to take risks. Forty years later, a life like all the lives she saw around her (imagined around her) was once again what she wanted but wasn't going to get.

When they met, when they married, Carter was a manager at a company that made vents and rain gutters and chimney caps for big construction projects. The construction sector, he called it, getting vital real life experience before he went for his MBA. He said that a career in manufacturing was something to be proud of, and he was almost eloquent when he talked about putting on a hard hat and hearing protection and learning his way around the factory floor.

Nina's job was in the entertainment sector, because she was a post production coordinator at a post production house. "It's a start," Carter said, encouragingly, on their first date. "Good for you."

That date was in a divey Mexican seafood restaurant that Carter had heard about at the factory. Piñatas—fantastic birds and mythical beasts and copyright-infringing comic-book characters—hung from the ceiling. The shrimp were served with their little legs still attached and the salsas and moles had complicated flavors unlike anything either of them—both white, with Midwestern roots—had ever tasted. They'd loved all of it. They'd imagined a wide variety of restaurants, with or without piñatas, in their futures. Now, Carter refused to eat out.

Why? what went wrong?

Nina moved from the entertainment sector, where jobs were scarce and harassment rampant, to the retail sector, which, except for the decrease in harassment, she liked less. Then she did the mom thing, which she liked a lot. Carter stayed too long at that first job and not long enough in the next, which was, in the lingo of the times but for reasons Nina never understood, not a good match. (His co-workers disliked him for his ambition, which he didn't bother to hide, and because—bookstore incident aside—he had poor social skills and no small talk.) He got promotions and raises when he worked for a hot tub manufacturer, but that business collapsed after it paid a huge damage award to an employee whom the owner had, unbeknownst to Carter, slept with and retaliated against. A job with a furniture business required frequent, arduous trips to China. A family owned business that made food service equipment needed a manager for the Los Angeles facility until a family member was ready to take over, but not longer. The MBA never happened.

By then, by the food service equipment job, Carter was sixty and going nowhere, resentful of his bad luck and blind to his bad choices. (A person can learn how to make small talk.) He developed an eagle eye for Nina's faults—her speeding tickets, her vanity, her insistence that her co-worker's partner's art show might have merit. The way she'd wanted to stay home with their kids, then bitched about what the interruption did to her career. "All those other people were putting in the work," he'd tell her. "They were learning their trade and creating value for their employers while you were finger painting and wiping noses. Why wouldn't they get hired, over you?"

It was cruel but accurate. She'd gotten her post-stay-at-home-mom jobs by leaving the PTA off her resume and lying about the date of her college degree and kept them by faking a cheerful attitude, but even in the retail sector, there were employees who'd developed skills and who gave a damn, and who spent none of their work time thinking about the pleasure of finger paint and cute baby noses. They created more value for their employers than she ever would.

At sixty-two, Carter had declared himself retired. Then it got worse. A shirt which was delivered without its full complement of buttons had to be returned to Macy's, so off he went to the mall. He took the stairs from the parking lot's top level, slipped on a meaty white gardenia petal fallen from someone's birthday flowers, and fell. He broke his leg, also his phone, which had been in his hand, because he'd been looking up the price of the shirt. He wanted to be credited the full price, not the sale price.

He was in that stairwell for half an hour until someone else decided to show his vigor by taking the stairs instead of the better-populated and regularly maintained escalators. (The flower recipient, leaving her shift at Macy's an hour earlier, had taken the stairs not to show vigor but because escalators gave her vertigo.) Carter spent the time crying from the very considerable pain and cursing himself for his clumsiness. "Can't you fucking watch where you're going?" he said out loud, to himself, echoing things said to him when he was a child. "Can't you fucking walk down a fucking flight of stairs?"

After the accident, he lost his confidence. He no longer trusted himself to keep his feet on the ground.

"It hits some people like that," the orthopedist told Nina with a shrug, after she begged him to talk to Carter, who wouldn't listen to her but who she hoped would listen to a scolding from a man. *Some old people*, the orthopedist meant. "He'll get over it." *And it's not my problem if he doesn't.* Nina heard the italics, which were loud.

Carter didn't get over it. He liked having Nina do everything for him. That was what she thought, though the doctors in the next round of doctors had a more sympathetic and enlightened attitude and different diagnoses. Anxiety, depression, mild agoraphobia. When the doctors labelled Carter's problems, Nina got a label, too: caregiver.

It was a tough job. Everyone knew that. Everyone knew that she'd get frustrated, fatigued, sometimes even angry, all best addressed in a support group, if there was a support group for people whose spouses had given up. Still, even though everyone felt sorry for her, everyone expected her to care-give, and everyone expected her to feel compassion, because the label meant that Carter's problems weren't his fault and weren't his to solve. (Was there a support group for people whose spouses lacked compassion?)

She wondered: what if everyone knew that Carter had stopped loving her long ago? That he'd mocked her and derided her? That he'd gotten nasty, even though nastiness wasn't on the official list of symptoms? Would that change everyone's mind about compassion? Probably not.

Suppose she said that he'd misrepresented himself as someone who could cope? Suppose she said that she'd been cheated? Everyone would laugh, because no one was married to the person they thought they'd married, and if you looked at it that way, everyone had been cheated. He'd suffered defeats. So what? Who hadn't?

Carter's sister was the only outlier. "Just stop taking care of him," Kristy said, when Nina turned to her for help. "He'll figure it out." But Kristy had been single her whole life and had never seemed happy about that, or anything else. Nina, in contrast, had loved, been loved, made vows. She'd pressed her naked body into Carter's naked body, elicited his moans, washed the sheets they'd marked with their commingled fluids.

She'd lived on his earnings and stayed silent when she saw him going off track—partly to avoid conflict, partly because she'd been jealous during his periods of success, and mostly because she was busy with the children, who were a lot more fun than he was. Nina knew that if she stopped taking care of Carter, if she left him, she'd have behaved too terribly even for herself.

(Kristy had done the moans/sheets/naked body thing, but she'd stopped herself from making the kind of mistake she thought Nina had made. What's the difference between a man and a savings bond? That was her joke, and the answer was, A savings bond matures. In Kristy's opinion, Carter had had it easy—the greater share of their mother's love, a wife to take care of him, two nice kids. Yes, he was old now—they both were—but it wasn't too late for him to step up. It was also true that Nina had always been something of a whiner.)

Nina drank her bitter coffee and ate her tasty cinnamon doughnut and brooded. She was only a few blocks from the seafood restaurant where she and Carter had had their first date. She wasn't interested in finding out whether it was still there.

(Omar was manning the grill at an upscale burger joint in the Valley, sweating like an animal in the kitchen's OSHA-violating ventilation-lacking heat and thinking about his truck, his two jobs, and his baba's baklava. The burger joint was so close to Nina's house that he could have given her a ride home and been at work on time. Not that he knew that. Not that the information would have changed anything.)

(The doughnut store owner worried about the rent, kept his hand on his phone while he watched an ominous-looking group of young men stroll toward the open front door, and waited for the drunks.)

In a dark corner of Nina and Carter's apartment, his work light the only light, Carter bent over a miniature battleship, frightened, dizzy from his meds, plagued with thoughts he couldn't tame with any of his doctor's, his wife's, the internet's, suggestions: Unhappy. Unloved. Unlucky. Unhappy. Unloved. Unlucky. Unmanned.

Or Else Three: Telephone Pole

Nina's beloved pale-blue Honda was a goner. "We only need one car any-way," she told Carter. Meaning that she'd drive his big, glossy, American sedan to work, to the supermarket, to the art galleries she liked to visit on weekends. Meaning that Carter wasn't going anywhere anyway.

His car. Paid for by both of them—California's a community property state—but chosen by him when he was still active, still working. He'd researched the options, opened and closed doors, adjusted mirrors and moved driver's seats forward and back. "Plenty of legroom," he'd said happily, when he got to this particular model. The salesman agreed. "A good car for a taller fellow. You have a long commute?"

"Not too bad," Carter answered, though at that point he had a fairly long commute. He ran a finger over the shiny dashboard chrome, then flung his arm across the passenger seat, empty because Nina was outside, analyzing the price sticker. "Test drive?" the salesman asked hopefully.

Like driving a couch, that's what Nina thought, first time she drove the car. Poor turning radius, and you got no sense of the road. Now, she perversely loved it. She started taking Laurel Canyon to work though the freeway was faster, just for the pleasure of the swoops and curves. She'd leave the house early, beat the traffic, sing along to a Joni Mitchell CD while she navigated the narrow road.

Big, heavy, smooth, safe. The car had been cooped up in an apartment house garage for too long.

Laurel Canyon dumped her onto Crescent Heights, which took her to Wilshire, to work, but one summer morning, she headed west on Sunset instead. The road was open, the sun risen. She needed to see the ocean. She needed some kind of absolution, and a good breath of cool ocean air was as close as she was going to get, because she didn't deserve absolution.

As a child, Nina had decided that she wanted to be a good person, like the sisters in *Little Women* who learned to curb their temper and vanity and materialism so that they could love and be loved; like Laura in *Little House*, who refused to hold her sister's real doll in front of her own corncob doll, to avoid hurting the corncob doll's feelings. Well, little girls and their dolls, but Laura's sacrifice had meant something to Nina.

She'd wanted to be like those girls. She'd wanted to be like her parents, who were calm and kind, affectionate, generous to her and each other. (They were also repressed and timid and rather bored, but they died young, and Nina never knew much about their inner lives.)

Nina didn't always remember her childhood decision, but she didn't entirely forget it, either, because childhood's not so easily abandoned and because—face it—it's an honorable ambition.

                                    The Louisville Review

So, she wanted to be good. She wasn't good. Mostly, she didn't even try.

Just that morning, Carter had gotten up early, which was one of his goals and not easy for him, but she wasn't happy to hear him in the shower, see him at the breakfast table. She'd rather have been alone with the jolly TV news anchors, and she'd let it show. She'd barely said "good morning," when he said "good morning." She'd snapped at him when he spilled a bag of coffee and hadn't governed her face when he said that he'd go out and buy more. He'd seen her disbelief. Her contempt; and it wasn't just that morning. It was chronic. It was who she'd become.

He deserved more. Everyone did, but Carter especially, because when you married someone, when you told them that it was safe to forsake all others, you took their happiness into your care. She had to do better by Carter.

She had to do better in general or she'd be snapping at people at work again. Lay-offs loomed, and when they happened, the least well-liked person was the one who'd get the axe. She was older than the rest of them. She had to remind them of their loving grandmas, not their mean moms.

The beach might do it; might refresh her and rejuvenate her and inspire her, so that she could be a decent person at work, a decent wife to Carter. So that she could be proud of herself. They couldn't afford two rents.

Carter, on new meds, ventured out. He had rubber-soled shoes, a rubber-tipped cane. He had a sun hat, a light jacket, and a goal, a Starbucks a few blocks away.

One block. Two. He'd cross Ventura at the light, and speaking of light, being outside was different. A kitchen chair on their tiny, one-chair balcony was nice, kept him from getting rickets, or so his doctor joked, but actual outdoor sunshine and breezes, the scrawny pink and white impatiens in someone's yard, a kid's red bike in a driveway, a glimpse of a woman reading in a cushioned wicker chair in a back yard—that was something else. Something much better.

On Ventura, a bit winded, Carter rested on a bus bench. "You ok?" a sweet-faced younger woman asked. It was more kindness than Nina had directed to him all year—except for the time when he'd had a fever and she'd brought him aspirin and water and had the old expression on her face, the one that said that she cared.

I didn't promise— he thought, though he'd made promises. *It's not my fault*—though some of it was. *No one's life turns out like they thought it would.* Which is true.

A mile down the street, a small truck was gathering speed. A drill rig—the driver drilled foundations for a living—was attached to the truck with hydraulics and chains, but despite what the driver thought, the rig wasn't securely attached. When the truck took a curve, then bounced into and out of a large pothole, the rig swung out and hit a telephone pole. Which snapped. Which fell.***

Like in a movie, Carter thought, watching the pole descend. He and Nina had loved disaster movies—earthquakes, volcanos—especially the ones set in L.A., predicting the end of a city where, back then, it was cheap to shoot and where the principals could sleep in their own beds. "Name! That! Location!" he'd say as some intersection or doughnut store or lush residential street was destroyed, and they'd laugh.

When the pole snapped, the well-known time-slowing effects of impending awfulness allowed him to think, *movie*, but time didn't slow enough for him to laugh. It took seconds for the pole to fall, and when it did, it was all over for Carter and for the kindly woman next to him.

Out in Malibu, Nina felt a burst of energy, which she attributed to the ocean air. *I can do this*, she thought. *I can be a good wife. A good person.*

Later that morning, she was surprised by the enormity of the grief that enveloped her. That never left her. Plus, the loss of identity. (Martyr.) Plus the shame. Life had provided her with a challenge—no, with an opportunity. She had not risen to it, and now she never would.

* Apologies to whoever has this license plate.
** Thanks to Jalopnik and its commenters for the car jokes.
*** A similar accident, minus the pothole, actually happened in Los Angeles County in the 1980s.

Robert Boucheron

Joseph Happ

The youngest of twelve, Joseph Happ was born as the family traveled upriver through the Shenandoah Valley, a wilderness in 1732. His parents Dietrich and Elfrieda belonged to a pietist sect called the Movement. Brothers and sisters by blood and faith, they moved in amphibious ox-drawn wagons made in Conestoga, Pennsylvania. Shaped like boats, covered with canvas on hoops, the wagons floated across rivers. Women and children rode as in a ferry, while men on horses and cattle waded.

The first ripple of a wave of German-speaking folk, the Happs came with little in the way of land deeds, certificates, and licenses. We would call them undocumented immigrants. Settlers who arrived a few years later and found the Happs on the spot called them squatters. Lawsuits and cash payments led to recognition of the status quo. Still, the early history of the area depends on oral tradition, not verifiable records.

The family caravan halted to rest for the night under a great oak tree. Nine months pregnant, Elfrieda Happ climbed down from the wagon and felt a birth pang. She lay on the ground and dozed. The weather was dry and warm. The month was June, and her labor lasted the few hours from dusk to dawn.

"I dreamed of a baby, and delivery came overnight," she said.

For lack of a cradle or any other furniture, Elfrieda laid the infant in a hollow formed by the roots of the oak tree. She then stood tall in the morning sun, spread her arms, and announced this was the spot ordained for them to inhabit. Her husband Dietrich had already yoked the team of oxen. Despite his passionate appeals to other family members, Elfrieda refused to budge. They set about erecting a log cabin. With sheds tacked on, surrounded by a fenced garden, a barn, a smokehouse, and so forth, this became the homestead of the Happs.

Elfrieda and her female kin revered the oak tree as the genius of the place. They kept pigs away, and someone hung a rope swing from a branch. In a ritual that smacked of the pagan past, the women tied ribbons around the trunk, poured milk and honey at the base, held hands in a circle, and chanted a short rhyme:

> *Mächtig' Eiche der Kindergeburt,*
> *Ewig bleibe grün' am Ort.*

Mighty oak of the infant birth,
Stay forever green on earth.

Last in seniority, Joseph was his mother's pet. To his older sisters, he was a living doll, then an educational prop for their future role as mothers, and finally a chore. A healthy infant, he was an active crawler and an early walker. He escaped the eyes of his elders, busy with tasks, and got into the forest. As he came to no harm, the family allowed him to wander. The toddler came to know trees and herbs, animals and birds, streams and hills, storm and calm. Elfrieda called him a *Naturkind*, a child of nature, protected by unseen forces.

At night, seated beside the glowing hearth, Elfrieda kissed the little boy's bruises and patched his clothes torn by briars. In the morning, she stuffed his pockets with things to eat, murmured a blessing, and waited. Day by day, Joseph strayed farther. By sunset he returned safe and sound. Often he surprised her with something he found in the woods: a fox kitten, a rare fungus, or an interesting pebble.

"What is it, Mama?" he asked.

Elfrieda told him if she knew. But if the thing was beyond her ken, she pretended to be angry.

"Why do you try my patience, naughty boy, when you know quite well?"

This became their private game.

By the age of seven, Joseph made his way alone to a native village. The Quidnunc tribe was an outlier of the Algonquin who occupied the eastern Atlantic coastal region. Here they came into conflict with the Monacan Sioux and the Iroquois, who expanded aggressively from the north. Tribal warfare was constant and savage. The Quidnunc were ready to strike a deal when the Happs arrived, steeped in doctrines of harmony and peace. Dietrich and his brothers met with tribal elders, smoked a ceremonial pipe, and agreed to provide mutual aid in case of attack. At other times, each side would mind their own business.

In their raids, the natives often abducted women and children. They made no exception for white settlers, and the captive's tale looms large in early American literature. Joseph turned the tables. The Quidnunc did not know what to make of the white boy who calmly wandered into their midst. He was fearless and wily as one of their own, who accepted him as a playmate, even a ringleader. The women fed Joseph. They worried that his mother would miss him and told him to go home. Instead, he came and went as he pleased. He charmed them with his antics, and he picked up the language. He stole trinkets from each side to give to the other. In a bid to tame him, the Quidnunc adopted Joseph into the Opossum Clan, a distinction he proudly claimed in later life.

Unlike the stock image of the taciturn warrior and the mute squaw, the Quidnunc were incorrigible gossips, much like present-day inhabitants. And like many today, Dietrich Happ was a lay preacher, compelled to take the gospel to complete strangers. The Quidnunc sat on the ground and listened politely. He rattled on in German, and Joseph provided a rough translation.

The natives said that Jesus must be a shaman, since he healed the sick and communicated with spirits exactly as their shamans did. His passion on the cross they interpreted as the torture a captive warrior must inevitably endure. The way he called God a father struck them as natural, since they did the same. But to Dietrich's chagrin, none could be persuaded to convert.

Like other natives, the Quidnunc lacked immunity to diseases brought from Europe. After 1750, through population loss, migration to the west, and astute blending in, they disappeared as an ethnic group. They bequeathed the name of Quicquid Creek, a few dialect words that trip up outsiders, and a pot-au-feu made with rabbit and squirrel, like Brunswick stew. They revered Afton Mountain, and their village lay on its western slope. The precise site of the village is in dispute, and the mountain's original name is lost. In the mid-1800s, after the railroad blasted its way through, people referred to a mail stop as Afton, and the name stuck.

As he entered his teens, Joseph resisted Dietrich's efforts to normalize his behavior. He learned basic farm tasks and the rudiments of reading, writing, and arithmetic. He sang well, and when a violin came into his hands, he learned to play simple tunes. But he spoke German with an accent, threw in native words and phrases, and played fast and loose with the truth. He shirked as many chores as he could, and he disappeared for days at a time in the wilderness. His father called him a *Taugenichts*, or good-for-nothing.

Like all the Happ children, Joseph absorbed the essential facts of the Christian religion. He was good by nature and full of spirit. Everyone admitted as much. But at the proper age, he balked at a confession of faith and confirmation. In these vital matters of church doctrine and discipline, Dietrich threw up his hands.

"Elfrieda indulges her baby," he said to the meeting, "and the Quidnunc fill his head with nonsense. He will follow his own nose and come to ruin."

By the time Joseph reached manhood at age eighteen, his father had passed to the heavenly kingdom. His brothers and sisters had married and moved away. The young man still lived with his mother on the rump of land that remained after divisions for inheritance, the few acres that were to be his portion. Elfrieda had reached the age of sixty. An old woman for that era, and a grandmother many times over, she kept the garden, while Joseph tended the gristmill his father had built. He also ferried people across Quicquid Creek at seasons of high water. But he came and went with a casual disregard for time and money. The names of farmer, miller, and ferryman were a loose fit. He was still a good-for-nothing.

It would be interesting to know what Joseph Happ looked like. A lively youth, he may have been a handsome man, but no portrait has come down to us. He could not sit still long enough for a painter. His granddaughter Hilda described him in old age as dry and leathery from a life lived in the open. Her verbal sketch says he was thin, restless, of moderate height, with hair like dirty flax, and blue eyes that stared right through you. Unlike the people he moved among, stout farmers and their stout wives, bowed under a burden of work and sin, he possessed the bodily grace of an athlete, the natives' habit of stealth, and their trick of turning up beside you. He had a boyish smile and uncanny senses of sight, hearing, and smell.

"I could detect a freshly baked pie before it went in the oven," he said.

If the patch of sand and gravel left to Joseph was poor soil for cultivation, only good for grazing cattle, it lay in the fertile plain of the Shenandoah. The climate was mild, rainfall was ample, and wildlife was abundant. Most important, a wagon trail or dirt road, a north-south route that may have begun as a deer track, crossed the creek at the mill. Another road connected to Rockfish Gap in the Blue Ridge, several miles to the east.

"Family and neighbors were blind to things that I saw as plain as day," he said. "From years of wandering and acquaintance with the natives, I possessed something better than a farm. I had a location."

Scotch-Irish and Welsh immigrants poured into the valley from the north. English settlers from Piedmont and Tidewater streamed through the mountain gap. Speakers of English were bound to outnumber the German-speaking folk. With an eye and ear to the future, Joseph added a third language to his repertoire. He quizzed travelers for news, bade new arrivals welcome, and translated on the spot for those who needed directions or wanted to buy and sell. Trade, he saw, had a life of its own. Though never very literate, Joseph was a great talker and a keen listener. Stirred by accounts of settlers on the move and cities sprouting in the wilderness, he would create one.

In the spring of 1750, on a flat shelf of land beside his mill on Quicquid Creek, Joseph hired a young surveyor to stake a small grid of streets, the usual layout for a frontier settlement. The existing road became Main Street where the town embraced it. As an afterthought, he marked a block in the middle "for public use." The surveyor was doing similar work for Lord Fairfax to the north around Winchester and in Rappahannock County. His original plat is lost, but a letter protesting the overdue bill survives in the collection of the Historical Society. Penned in the cursive for which he would become famous, the letter is signed by George Washington.

An early instance of moonlighting, the incident shows that the Father of His Country, who would later determine the site of the national capital, was the author of the plan of Hapsburg. The two young men discovered they were born the same year. Washington had an edge, being four months older, eight inches taller, and the son of a rich planter. He pretended to be indifferent, but young Happ felt a mystic bond of brotherhood. He would follow his friend's career with interest, fervently support the patriot cause, and suffer a grievous loss when President Washington died at the end of the century.

Town lots went up for sale. Takers were few, and some were speculators who left the lots vacant. Early letters mention the place as Happ's Ford, Happ's Mill, and Hapsborough. In time, despite a similarity to the Austrian royal house, the name Hapsburg prevailed. With the help of someone who spoke better English, possibly a circuit-riding Anglican minister, Joseph wrote a "Prospectus" for the town. It was printed as a handbill for distribution to potential settlers. One copy survives. A hand-colored woodcut shows an idyllic scene of a mill, a cluster of houses, foliage, and a steeple. In the foreground, a smartly dressed couple rides in a two-horse buggy. Under this is the text:

Exceptional opportunity for those who wish to make a fresh
start! A new city arises on the banks of Quicquid Creek, an important
tributary of the Shenandoah, which debouches to the upper reaches
of the Potomac River. Navigation is thereby assured year-round, and a
brisk commerce will inevitably follow. In addition to access by water,
the town has admirable connections by land, as it lies athwart the Great
Wagon Road, and on a busy way from a gap in the Blue Ridge to points
west. Prosperous farms surround the city. A mill has been established,
surely the first of many. Lots in all districts are available, but interested
buyers are advised to hurry, as the most desirable will be the first to go.
The proprietor may be found at Happ's Mill or in the near vicinity.

Joseph continued to operate the mill. To fulfill a verbal promise made to
clinch a sale, he built a shaky wooden bridge to replace the ferry. Floods
destroyed the bridge more than once. A stone span would replace it in
1858. A few frame houses arose, small and one-story, loosely scattered
on dirt lanes. Fences ran every which way. Yards were bare. There was no
steeple. The fledgling town looked nothing like the handbill.

The largest house was a general store and tavern with bedrooms
upstairs. G. Williker's was a popular stop for travelers, a landmark for
many years. In the next century, it would gain renown as a hotel, and
loyal patrons would transform the name into a common expression.
Joseph made daily visits to the tavern.

"I saw the evil effects of liquor on the Quidnunc. I also saw the value
of standing a treat. Drink loosens the tongue, and talk is business."

Seven years after the town was conceived, Elfrieda expressed a
dying wish that Joseph should marry. Anyone would do, but a cousin
was available. Anna Pfaffenberger was a modest person, the youngest
daughter of the house. At twenty-five, she was the same age as he and
ripe for the picking. Joseph made no objection.

Elfrieda gave Anna the only piece of jewelry she possessed, a silver
locket on a chain. She had brought it with her on the journey to Virginia.
Her mother had brought it from her native Germany and bestowed it as
a bridal gift. Elfrieda knew nothing of its origin, except that it was old.
It may be the same silver locket passed down through several generations
and now exhibited in the Lyceum. Oval in shape and embossed with
leaves and flowers in arabesque, it bears no date or maker's mark. The
wedding took place, and Elfrieda died happy.

The young couple moved into the old log house. Children followed, the house filled again, and Anna tended the garden Elfrieda had planted. The waterwheel turned, and the millstones ground. Traffic grew steadily, as more and more farmers brought their grain and took away sacks of flour. But just as he was a reluctant miller, Joseph was a part-time husband. By the third child, Anna understood that she would have to be both mother and father of the household. She urged the firstborn son, August, to grow into a responsible adult as soon as possible.

By the 1770s, news of revolutionary events reached the frontier town in the Shenandoah Valley. Joseph took a keen interest, but he was now in his forties and a family man, as Anna firmly reminded him. When war broke out, going off to fight was out of the question. Instead, as a well-known character, Joseph got himself elected to the Virginia legislature. He made annual trips to the capital at Williamsburg, where he hobnobbed with men of superior wealth and education—plantation owners, merchants, and lawyers. They did more than follow the rules, they made the rules. Joseph made friends.

Toward the end of 1778, General Washington's army camped at Valley Forge, Pennsylvania. Joseph heard of their hardships and hunger and decided there was something he could do. His son August was old enough to manage the mill, and his wife Anna was resigned to his absences. Chores were few in midwinter. The dirt roads were frozen and passable. He filled a wagon with provisions, drove it to Valley Forge, a distance of almost three hundred miles, and arrived in January. Along the way, Joseph talked up his project. Sympathetic people gave him free lodging and fodder for the oxen. Children waved, shouted hurrah, and followed the wagon for as much as a mile.

Washington was surprised and pleased by the donation. Joseph reminded him they had met in the Shenandoah twenty-eight years before. The general then clasped his hand warmly and made a short and gracious speech.

"On behalf of the Continental Army, Mr. Happ, I offer most sincere thanks. A previous engagement makes it impossible for me to linger and reminisce, as is my earnest desire, but I cordially invite you to dine at the officers' mess. And you must visit the quartermaster for whatever is needed in the way of repairs to your wagon and personal equipment."

Joseph did so, stayed overnight in a log hut, one of hundreds built by the soldiers as winter quarters, and began his journey home the next day.

The adventure was a substitute for military service. Joseph had nothing to show for it but an empty wagon and a pair of worn-out boots, but he turned it to account in the next few years. In 1780, the state capital moved up the James River to Richmond. Population growth in the west encouraged the formation of a new county. Joseph wanted his town to be recognized and placed at the center. He lobbied hard for home. His reputation was high, and he was a native Virginian, he pointed out. His fellow delegates found him inescapable. In 1783, the same year the Treaty of Paris ended the Revolutionary War, the legislature created Quidnunc County, named for the native tribe, and it granted a charter to the town of Hapsburg as the new county seat.

Political status brought success at last. After thirty-three years of nothing much, Hapsburg boomed. Construction of a courthouse began at once. Nothing is known about this structure, which may have been of logs, beyond a complaint that it was drafty. It was soon replaced by a wood frame structure of which a sketch survives. The sketch shows a simple quadrilateral. In 1832, citizens raised money through a lottery to erect a chaste temple of red brick with columns of buff stucco. This is the building we see today. The block in which it stands is the one reserved from the start for public use. Planted with elm trees, boxwood, and crape myrtle, with an expanse of neatly mowed grass, this green space attracted law offices, churches, and a public library to its perimeter. Court Square is now acknowledged to be jewel of urban design.

As well as for legal business, Hapsburg developed as a market for agricultural products—grain, lumber, wool, flax, beef, cattle hides for leather, and poultry feathers for stuffing. The town acquired a tannery, a brickyard, a pottery, and a *Tischler,* a woodworker or cabinetmaker. Mills multiplied along Quicquid Creek, as the prospectus had promised. August Happ, now in charge of the family grist mill, enlarged the operation. He added a new type of waterwheel and up-to-date mechanical works. August also married Gertrude Wildfang, the daughter of a local farmer. At this time, they built or rebuilt the fieldstone farmhouse known as Meadow Grange.

Joseph Happ was elected the first mayor of Hapsburg, an office he held for fifteen years. Improbably enough for a child of nature and good-for-nothing, he became the first citizen. When the frame courthouse was built, it included an office for the town, and Joseph shifted his base of activity there. For the first time in his life, he had a regular place of business, with a desk, a lamp, and a cabinet for important papers. Old habits were hard to break, however. Mayor Happ had little interest in the formal trappings of office. He gladly let the clerk take over. The ornate Town Hall that stands today under its Baroque dome was built a century later. Artistic in the style of the 1890s, it adds a note of bombastic splendor.

Joseph continued to haunt the tavern on Main Street, where an armchair was shown many years after as the spot in which he had met fellow citizens, received letters and payments, dictated replies, and entertained visitors with stories. In the streets of his town, he walked and talked by the hour. He buttonholed men, saluted women, and teased young children. He strolled on the banks of Quicquid Creek and hailed *batteaux*, the shallow boats used for cargo.

"My wandering days were over," he said, "but my legs still had the itch."

Anna Happ, as Joseph's long-suffering wife, rose to the first rank among the women of Hapsburg. She declined the honor of being called a lady, and she continued to dress in the plain homespun skirts and linen cap of a Mennonite housewife. Despite common knowledge, she insisted that Joseph had always been her mainstay, her rod and staff. All she wanted in life was for him and their children to be happy.

The Happ homestead was originally situated at the edge of town, where Main Street turns to cross the bridge. By the 1790s, the town had absorbed it. Joseph and Anna sold the property and moved to Meadow Grange to live with their son's family. In the next century, the old house was torn down for commercial development. The oak tree may have decayed and fallen by this time, or an ignorant owner may have cut it down. Two acorns preserved in the Historical Society are supposed to have dropped from its branches. Gibson's Corner Store now occupies the site, as a historical marker in the storefront affirms.

After making do with itinerant clergy for many years, in 1792 the English inhabitants, who could not abide the Scottish Presbyterians, the German Pietists, the newfangled Baptists, or other religious riffraff, organized a congregation in the established faith of Virginia, now called the Episcopal Church. Though nominally Christian, Joseph was independent, a political weak spot. Still, he was the leading citizen and largest landowner. The new Episcopal rector approached Joseph and offered him a deal.

"Your social position makes the condition of your soul more than a private affair between yourself and the Creator. It is also a matter of public concern. I am informed, Mr. Happ, that you are sixty years old. If you feel moved to donate a building lot, we will welcome you into the fold, no questions asked.

Joseph signed over an acre on a low ridge on the eastern edge of what was then the built-up area. Hill Street was added to the town plan, and St. Giles Episcopal Church was completed in 1794. Today this solid fieldstone structure is the oldest house of worship in continuous use. An adjacent rectory was built some years later of the same stone, with Gothic details. Still later, a wrought-iron fence around the churchyard united a harmonious ensemble. In the 1800s, Hill Street attracted wealthy residents in noteworthy examples of Greek Revival, Italianate, and Victorian architecture. St. Giles now stands at the apex of fashion.

In December 1799, news of the death of Washington at Mount Vernon affected the whole country and Joseph in particular. He took to bed. Attended by family and people of the town who came to pay their respects, he rambled through memories of the past and made predictions. To pass the time and set the record straight, he dictated a "Prophecy" to his granddaughter Hilda. Quick-witted, she had learned to read and write. This handwritten document, preserved in the Historical Society, is the source of much of what we know. Hilda set down what she heard with no attempt at order or plausibility. In some passages she seems to translate on the fly, from German to English, or that may be the way the old man talked. His vision for the town is rosy.

"The people will prosper happily ever after."

Joseph Happ died soon after this, in the year 1800. He was buried in the churchyard of St. Giles, where many descendants would join him in time. As befits the man, his gray limestone memorial is not the largest or the most elaborate. A stubby obelisk on a plain cube bears his dates and the following inscription:

Here Lies Joseph Happ,
Native Son, Patriot,
Founder of Hapsburg.
All Flesh Must Die,
Yet Bear in Mind,
The Last Shall Be First.

Mary Popham

Book Review: *Journeyman*, by Rick Neumayer

When hitchhiking buddies, Pate and Stan, young men at difficult junctures in their lives, set out on the road to Haight-Ashbury in June, 1971, they know that the Summer of Love took place in 1967, but surely, four years later, some of those 100,000 flower children are still there, searching for a new life, or hiding from an old one. It sounds like the perfect solution for the atmosphere of uncertainty they face during the horror of the Vietnam War. "King and both Kennedys are dead, Nixon's in the White House, and the Beatles have broken up, anything and nothing seems possible."

What do these young bearded men have in common, and why do they burn bridges in Louisville to travel 2,000 miles? Pate Merwin has worked as a teacher of predominately black students in the West End and recently as a church janitor. Stan Hicks has been in the Navy, but is now against the war, and quits a monotonous job in a cigarette factory. Author Rick Neumayer deftly reveals both of their personalities, backgrounds, worries, and dreams in this story of learning about the self, as Pate and Stan meet various types of people throughout their journey. By writing alternating chapters that begin in present-tense as the story opens, then switch to past-tense with an account of eight months earlier, the back stories catch up to the present when the guys reach San Francisco.

The two men are acquaintances in Louisville, and though they don't know each other well, they share an apartment. Soon Pate has a live-in girlfriend, but they have difficulties as a couple. He hasn't sufficient income to start family life, and he isn't ready to be a father to her son. The stress of teaching in a school system that cannot meet the needs of difficult to control students, who can barely read, contributes to his desire to join his friend and leave it all behind. While Pate has recently avoided being drafted into the senseless war, Stan, equally adrift, has done his time in the service, but he flounders from job to job and wanders from one casual sex partner to another. He searches for reasons to live.

Pate and Stan are great readers. Pate, the teacher, likes Kurt Vonnegut. Stan also enjoys deep discussions, favoring the spiritual nature of the recluse of Walden Pond. He notes, "Thoreau believed we can't begin tounderstand ourselves until we're lost." He seems to aim toward dangerous paths, perhaps his way to gain self-awareness.

Less daring of the two, Pate worries that Stan's behavior is too risky. More selective of the drivers who stop for them, Pate ruminates, "There are rules for hitchhiking, perhaps not written down, but rules just the same, and only fools ignore them." As a pair, however, each has an underlying know-how and compassion which serve them well. They abandon a sleepy truck driver, are threatened by rednecks in a Kansas diner, and put up with a traveling salesman whose advice is good even though he is a bore. "You've got to like people," the talkative man says. Stan tells him they are Communists and they are immediately dumped. But sometimes the need to rest their feet or get out of the rain prevails over common sense safety rules. With outstretched thumbs and the hubris that only the young can employ, they continue their travels.

Rick Neumayer is a skillful teacher and writer, a man interested in details that others might miss. He creates his characters with flaws and weaknesses along with their intelligence, abilities, charm, and kindness. His men appreciate the side trips: "As the sharp-edged mountains slowly fade and the purple velvet sky turns gray, we stroll through the sage-brush." Memories sometimes sweeten the present: one of them remembers the smell of a woman's clean hair; the other, the hint of coconut-scented suntan lotion that women smear on each other. Smoking a joint, Pate notices the enhanced beauty. "The light has changed. Now the desert's warm browns, golden corals, and muted reds appear even more vivid. Whatever the cause—an aesthetically minded God or a jubilant and random Nature—it's stunningly magnificent."

A trek on foot, by plane, train, or automobile is always a journey of self-discovery. Neumayer's *Journeyman* is part of a grand tradition of travelers-seekers: Odysseus wanders throughout the world, seemingly unable to return home to his wife and son. Is it a longing for adventure that keeps him away? Chaucer invents a mixed set of travelers: The Knight who fights only religious wars; The Squire who considers himself a ladies' man; The Prioress whose emphasis is on her appearance; The Monk who prefers the outdoor life to the monastery; The Friar who knows the taverns better than his parish; The Wife of Bath who has been on five pilgrimages and also has been married five times.

Our Journeymen admire Ken Kesey, a writer and counterculture hero. He and his followers, the Merry Pranksters, are noted for the lengthy, cross-country road trip they took in the summer of 1964. Pate and Stan have romanticized the group, as they like the idea of being hippies and look forward to communal living with the sharing of food and love. They draw comfort from the notion of turning on, tuning in, and dropping out, but their dreams take on a different life than they expect and bring results they could not have foreseen.

Pate and Stan share the restlessness of many wanderers/seekers. Perhaps the young men of Neumayer's creation are most like Steinbeck's Joad family, betrayed, however, not so much by the forces of nature—an unrelenting dust bowl—but by a culture that embraces war all too readily and ignores the needs of many of its citizens. Perhaps *Journeyman* suggests, ultimately, that salvation lies in the redemptive creativity of our own hands.

Cornerstone

work by writers K-12

Kieran Chung

Strangers and Ghosts

you danced with me in a darkened hall
filled with strangers and ghosts
candles cast our shadows long and thin,
spider legs knitting invisible threads
running tripwires by our ankles
then dissolving back into a patch of light
there was no music,
only hollow footsteps and the sound of breathing
a shadow fell across your face
and you shivered—
your beating heart
transformed into a sickly yolk
until we stepped back into the light
and you clung to me,
corporeal once more

our fingers intertwined,
tentative, then tighter
until the space between our skin vanished
it reminded me of summers long past,
climbing knotted oak branches,
the sun scorching our cheeks
bark cut into our fingers, but still we held on,
dancing around each other,
dancing with the shadows we cast
lost on the ground
so far below,
dancing together, immortal,
preserved in an endless sun

as it was then, it was now,
my footfalls sure, yours surer
the pace picked up
in a whirl of steps
as one by one, the dancers were swallowed

into their shadows, their ghosts
and we realized the evening had deepened
you met my eyes,
and we danced a little faster,
twirling away from the shadows that came for us,
stepping over the patches of inky black
that pooled and whispered at our feet
our desperation became the melody
to which we danced
we sought the light
but the candles climbed up the walls
to their own refuge in the vaulted ceiling
they left us on the ground, lost
so far below,
until the shadows pulled us in
our hearts turned to yolks
and splattered upon the pitch-black floor

we danced together, immortal,
with strangers and with ghosts

Sofia Dzodan

How Does the Sky Look?

The first sky I remember feeling was when I met my best friend
we were two and were drawn into inevitable dawn tinted in pink
lining my skin and lungs on the inside
I felt that pink (and some purple) of the sky slowly slide into me
spreading serenity from my breath to my bloodstream
it might seem odd to you that I remember that sky from when I was two
     years old
but I will tell you a secret: strongest skies can last lifetimes.

And as aging and time creep into me, I remember other skies
like the one I inhaled at times when mum and dad had those fights
covered in fat clouds creating catastrophic thunder in grey weather
that sky was more like an intruder when my mouth gaped for air
in a bleak winter day. It came with a sharp stab to my warm lungs.
This sky did not run in my bloodstream, it led my veins to collapse
It was like a storm bursting inside of me until I bleed it all out.

I can also recall orange tinted skies in sundown
there are plenty of these for each occasion of frantic passion
like in afternoons of theatre and poetry and art and literature
like in afternoons of lips intertwined in the hope of savoring more
     than flesh
when that sky swelled inside of my chest provoking intensity
my body became as solid as ever, pounding heartbeats contained.

Yet even if the atmosphere has the slight pleasure of instability
neither storm nor dawn nor sundown can last long luring my senses
when I look at it all from zero to seventeen
there is only one sky lining my skin within
some spongy white clouds and light water droplets allowed
around incandescent sunlight coming through, oh, lighter hues
it might be how much I grew in between carrying weight and giving
     care too

sweet voice saying thank you for it all reminds me how I
          gripped tight
a ruptured handle of flawless family. Could only hold on with
          unconditional love
above some lies about how everything was fine after secret sobbing
          surrendered
sky shows a kaleidoscope of rain and sun and dwindling days
          in a distance

I think my existence was meant to fix stuff in spite of the cuts I got
releasing rain then leaves a hole to let sun through
see my spirit now? A woman of strong senses, some say
but if you have seen me, my sky, my mind, and where my love lies
you would know my radiance is not a casualty.

Sofia Dzodan

Myself, My Basement

Only occasionally I go down to my basement
down where decaying photographs are stashed
in between memories stained in yellow and dark.
Only occasionally I think about that part of me
where it all seems sad and immoral and solely vice is stored
from its core down my throat filled with slim sin
I try to avoid. I don't like staying stuck in there for too long
where I remember all the things I hate about myself and how
I once did something wrong. Things that troubled me
made me stay locked up, reeking of melancholy and disgust
in between all thoughts that made my head hurt
in hollowing hostility: dizzy from distress, so now I digress.
Down in my basement
I may stay for too long looking at how
things hurt and hate. Please pinch me when I do
lift me up and take me away
because I do dwell too much on those tempting stairs
leading down there. It's not sane nor safe
so better stay away
at least until the moment in which
never-ending oblivion may take me down there
and doesn't allow me back up again.

Sofia Dzodan

Submerged in Water

2 a.m.
Stuck in between
my laptop in front of me
and my mind within
unraveling a series of thoughts that circle
my head and are laid out in front of me
even though they do not materialize

3 a.m.
I should sleep
no work is done yet I have not stopped since
I started. The more I try focus, the more I fail
and the more I feel feet against sand
rough and sweaty in the humid air that envelops me
a caress, a hushed wave sliding in
cold that comes to tickle my toes

4 a.m.
Still locked up in my room
trying to figure out why I am alive when someday I will die
or why seawater envelops me so perfectly
no wonder I float so ferociously
submerged in salty swell
wondering when will this end

5 a.m.
Lights off: at least try to get some sleep.
How? I am still clustered inside
confinement does me no favors
as air concentrates around me
it surrounds me, so heavy, I think it could condensate
rain atop my vicious head
wash out thoughts and take them away

in salty sea breeze
that makes my hair cling to my cheeks

6 a.m.
Sun is rising
I know it because I see light coming in the room
through the window
yet I still feel suspended in a sea
of scrutiny where I feel static yet
steady movement of thoughts like seaweed
undulating in the quiet current of water
it stays there, solid and unwavering
submerged deep inside the tide circling my brain

7 a.m.
Almost asleep
the current eases on my brain
as it prepares to stay still for a while.
My room becomes blurry
things in my mind get tangled with my bedsheets
I might have dozed off...

8 a.m.
My alarm goes off
another day of the same thing
starts again

Hannah Slayton

In Between Purgatory and You

I cut the food up
into little digestible bits,
something for your snake-skin belly to feel
down your gullet, down
the walls of our Virginia home, where you
have made a limbo
between six feet beneath the red and crumbling clay
and me, your daughter
red blood pulsing beneath the skin you made
one night so recklessly, so thoughtless as to plan
such a destructive act as a child.
You could not have thought of this then,
this space between us as you fade
with every doctor's visit, with every MRI
so slowly into the background of reality
that even I cannot see you
dripping from the spigot into the drain as a comfortable, small solace
between limbos,
between me and nothing,
or something else, depending on who you ask.
You have made our house a box
with a cat inside,
with the radium that is supposed to fix your brain inside,
with me inside
to feel you as you drip away
the useless seconds between now and the inevitable
conclusion.

Notes on Contributors

DONNA GAY ANDERSON is a playwright/lyricist currently collaborating with composer Theodore Christman on the musical, *Unfolded*, based on the life and work of *Susie Scott Krabacher*. Works include *High and Mighty, Shrimp and Crab* and *Formula One*. She has served as a contributing writer to Dramatists Magazine and MusicalWriters.com. MFA Spalding University. She and her husband live in swampy south Louisiana. www.donnagayanderson.com.

SIMON ANTON NIÑO DIEGO BAENA lives in the Philippines with his wife, Xandy. He is the author of the chapbook, *The Magnum Opus Persists in the Evening* (Jacar Press). His work has appeared, or will appear, in *The American Journal of Poetry, The Cortland Review, Osiris, North Dakota Quarterly, Gargoyle, The Bitter Oleander, Louisiana Literature, Phantom Drift,* and *The Inflectionist Review,* among others.

JIM BELLAR is an author, musician, and consultant based in the Nashville area. His short story titled "Mama, I Need Some Money!" is a chapter from his southern Gothic novel *The Deal*, about sex and extortion in a 1960's small town. Jim once opened for Americana legend Townes Van Zandt at The Bluebird Café and is co-writing a book about the importance of taking time off during college for experiential learning.

J. A. BERNSTEIN is the author of four published or forthcoming volumes, including a novel, *Rachel's Tomb* (New Issues, 2019), which won the Association of Writers & Writing Programs Award Series Prize; and a chapbook, *Desert Castles* (Southern Indiana Review Press, 2019), which won the Wilhelmus Prize. His stories, poems, and essays have appeared in *Washington Square, Kenyon Review Online, Boston Review*, and other journals. A Chicago native, he is an assistant professor of English and Director of Graduate Studies in English at the University of Southern Mississippi, as well as the fiction editor of *Tikkun*.

ROBERT BOUCHERON is an architect in Charlottesville, Virginia. His short stories and essays appear in *Bellingham Review, Fiction International, Flash Nonfiction, Food, Lowestoft Chronicle, Saturday Evening Post*, and other magazines.

MARGARITA CRUZ recently received her MFA in Creative Writing from Northern Arizona University. Vice President of the Northern Arizona Book Festival, she is currently a columnist for *Flagstaff Live!* and an assistant editor at Tolsun Books. Her works have been featured in *PANK, Chapter House Journal*, and the *Susquehanna Review.*

LESLIE DANIELS' first novel, *Cleaning Nabokov's House,* has been published in translation in four languages. The novel, now under option for film, fights the good fight of being both literary and funny. Daniels' stories and essays have appeared in numerous publications. She served as fiction editor of *Green Mountains Review,* currently teaches writing at the

Spalding University MFA program, and the Community of Writers at Squaw Valley. Leslie Daniels lives in Ithaca, New York.

GRANT DEAM holds a BA from Knox College and an MAT from Dominican University. He taught high school Spanish in Chicago before pursuing an MFA through Southern Illinois University Edwardsville. He currently is an adjunct faculty member at McKendree University and hosts the podcast *Writers in the World*.

LAINE DERR is a graduate of Northern Arizona University's MFA Creative Writing program. He believes in the transformative role of the arts, an opportunity for connection, for purpose. He has published interviews with Carl Phillips and Ross Gay, and is currently based in Rockville, Maryland.

JESSICA EVANS (Spalding University MFA '16) writes from Arlington, Virginia. Home is where she lays her head and has included some far-off distant lands. She's the EIC of *Twin Pies*, poetry editor for *Dress Blues*, and serves as a mentor for *Veteran's Writing Project*. Work is forthcoming in *LEON Literary*, *Outlook Springs*, *The Wild Hunt*, and elsewhere. Connect with her on Twitter @jesssica__evans

AMY L. FAIR is a West Virginia native and the daughter and granddaughter of steelworkers. She holds an MFA from Chatham University and is working on a nonfiction book about tattooed women in the early 1900s. Amy currently makes her home in rural Oregon, where she teaches at a small community college and plans to grow old without any grace whatsoever.

PETER GRANDBOIS is the author of twelve books, the most recent of which is *Everything Has Become Birds* (Brighthorse 2020). His poems, stories, and essays have appeared in over one hundred journals. His plays have been nominated for several New York Innovative Theatre Awards and have been performed in St. Louis, Columbus, Los Angeles, and New York. He is poetry editor at *Boulevard* magazine and teaches at Denison University in Ohio. You can find him at www.petergrandbois.com.

TOM C. HUNLEY is a professor in the MFA/BA programs at Western Kentucky University, where he has taught since 2003. He won the 2020 Rattle Chapbook Prize and the 2020 SmokeLong Quarterly AWP Microfiction Award. *What Feels Like Love: New and Selected Poems* is forthcoming in 2021 from C&R Press.

ANNA IDELEVICH is a scientist by profession, PhD, MBA, trained in the neuroscience field at Harvard University. She writes poetry for pleasure. Her books and poetry collections include *DNA of the Reversed River* and *Cryptopathos* published by the Liberty Publishing House, New York. We hope you will enjoy their melody, new linguistic tone, and a slight tint of an accent.

Marci Rae Johnson is a freelance writer and editor, and the poetry editor for WordFarm press. Her poems appear or are forthcoming in *Image, The Christian Century, Main Street Rag, The Collagist, Rhino, Quiddity, Hobart, Redivider, Redactions, The Valparaiso Poetry Review, The Louisville Review*, and *32 Poems*, among others. Her most recent book, *Basic Disaster Supplies Kit*, was published by Steel Toe Books.

Maxima Kahn's debut full-length collection of poems, *Fierce Aria*, was released by Finishing Line Press in May 2020. She has received fellowships and scholarships to the Vermont Studio Center and the Community of Writers. Having taught at the University of California, Davis Extension, she now teaches and blogs at BrilliantPlayground.com. You can find out more about her writing at MaximaKahn.com and get insider access to her creative process and new works at Patreon.com/MaximaKahn.

Kate Kaplan lives and works in Los Angeles. She graduated from Sarah Lawrence College, Northeastern Law School, and the MFA Program for Writers at Warren Wilson, and has published fiction in the *New England Review*, the *Santa Monica Review*, and other journals, and craft essays on using jokes in fiction in *Craft* and the *Fiction Writers' Review*.

Tyler King is a non-binary poet from Dayton, Ohio. They are the editor of Flail House Press and their work has appeared in *Ghost Heart Literary Journal, Indolent Books, Sonder Midwest*, and other places.

Angie Macri is the author of *Underwater Panther* (Southeast Missouri State University), winner of the Cowles Poetry Book Prize. Her recent work appears in *Arkansas International, The Laurel Review*, and *Zone 3*. An Arkansas Arts Council fellow, she lives in Hot Springs and teaches at Hendrix College.

Jen McConnell is a fiction writer and poet. Her work is forthcoming or has recently appeared in *The Louisville Review, Reflex Press, Vagabonds, What Rough Beast, The Harpoon Review*, and others. Her debut collection of short stories, *Welcome, Anybody*, was published by Press 53. In addition to her day job as a corporate copywriter, she is co-fiction editor and creative nonfiction editor for *The Bookends Review*. She holds an MFA in Creative Writing from Goddard College and a Pushcart Prize Nomination for her fiction. Read more at jenmcconnell.com.

Milica Mijatović is a Serbian poet and translator. Born in Brčko, Bosnia and Hercegovina, she relocated to the United States where she earned a BA in Creative Writing and English Literature from Capital University. She recently received her MFA in Creative Writing from Boston University and is a recipient of a Robert Pinsky Global Fellowship in Poetry.

John A. Nieves has poems forthcoming or recently published in journals such as: *North American Review, Crazyhorse, Southern Review, Harvard Review* and *Massachusetts Review*.

He won the Indiana Review Poetry Contest and his first book, *Curio*, won the Elixir Press Annual Poetry Award Judge's Prize. He is associate professor of English at Salisbury University and an editor of *The Shore Poetry*. He received his MA from University of South Florida and his PhD from the University of Missouri.

GREG PAPE is the author of *Four Swans, Animal Time, American Flamingo*, and several other books. He served as Montana Poet Laureate, 2007 to 2009. Professor Emeritus at University of Montana, he teaches in the MFA program at Spalding University's School of Creative and Professional Writing.

SIMON PERCHIK is an attorney whose poems have appeared in *Partisan Review, Forge, Poetry, Osiris, The New Yorker* and elsewhere. His most recent collection is *The Reflection in a Glass Eye* published by Cholla Needles Arts & Literary Library, 2020. For more information including free e-books and his essay, "Magic, Illusion and Other Realities," please visit his website at www.simonperchik.com. To view one of his interviews please follow this link https://www.youtube.com/watch?v=MSK774rtfx8

MARY POPHAM is a 2003 graduate of the Spalding MFA in Writing Program. Her novels set in Central Kentucky in the early 1900s are *Back Home in Landing Run* and *The Wife Takes a Farmer.* The final in the trilogy, *Emmalene of Landing Run,* is forthcoming. She has also published a collection of short stories, *Love is a Fireplace.*

DAVID ROMANDA lives in Kawasaki City, Japan. His work has appeared in *Gargoyle, Hawaii Review, The Main Street Rag, PANK,* and *Puerto del Sol.* David's chapbook, *I'm Sick of Pale Blue Skies,* is slated for publication in spring 2021.

KATERINA STOYKOVA is the author of several award-winning poetry books and the Senior Editor of Accents Publishing, where she has selected, edited, and published close to 80 poetry collections. She hosts the literary radio show Accents on WRFL 88.1FM. Katerina acted in the lead roles in the independent feature films *Proud Citizen* and *Fort Maria,* both directed by Thom Southerland. She splits her time between the coast of the Black Sea and the rolling hills of Kentucky. Katerina writes, lives and thinks in two languages.

LORI ANN STEPHENS is the author of *Song of the Orange Moons* and several books for young people, including *Novalee and the Spider Secret.* Her award-winning short stories have been published in *Glimmer Train Stories, The Chicago Tribune,* and other print-treasures. She lives in Richardson, Texas, and teaches writing at Southern Methodist University.

JASON TANDON is the author of four books of poetry including, *The Actual World* (Black Lawrence Press, 2019). His poems have appeared in many journals and magazines, including *Ploughshares, Prairie Schooner, Beloit Poetry Journal, North American Review,* and *Esquire.* He is a senior lecturer in the Arts & Sciences Writing Program at Boston University.

LAURIE WELCH earned an MFA in Poetry from the University of Nebraska. Her poems have appeared in *LA Review, Sugar House Review*, and others. She lives and teaches in Omaha.

STAN LEE WERLIN'S short stories and poetry have appeared in *Southern Humanities Review, Los Angeles Review, Sheepshead Review, Prime Number, Glassworks, Futures Trading, Soundings East, Saranac Review, Bacopa Literary Review, Zone 3, Gargoyle, Reunion, The Write Launch, Waymark*, and *Roanoke Review.* His humorous children's poetry has been published in numerous children's magazines and anthologies. He was a Harvard undergrad and received an MBA from The Wharton School. Twitter @natsnilrew

TAYLOR ZHANG is a teaching fellow at Columbia University, where she recently finished coursework for her MFA. She runs a small Risograph press (Choo Choo Press) that publishes literary zines and chapbooks with an emphasis on queerness, nostaligia, and states of liminality. Originally from Jackson, Mississippi, she now lives and works in Brooklyn, New York.

NOTES ON CONTRIBUTORS TO CORNERSTONE

KIERAN CHUNG is a 10th grader at Harvard-Westlake School in Los Angeles, California. The work of this group has been recognized by the Scholastic Writing Awards and published in their school's literary magazine and the CTY Lexophilia magazine. They also compose music and are working on a science fiction novel.

SOFIA DZODAN is a student aspiring to share her thoughts and ideas through verse. Having grown up reading poetry from highly influential writers, Sofia hopes that she can make an impact on other people the same way poets influenced and affected her life. She is a proud environmentalist and feminist seeking to make this world a little better one day.

HANNAH SLAYTON is a young writer based in Charlottesville, Virginia. She uses her work to explore loss and grief in unusual settings, and she continues to studying writing in her free time. When not writing, she can be found composing songs on her piano.

Rajasthan state in India has always been my favorite destination ever since I was a kid visiting my dad working there. Every city there inevitably has a glorious past and a beautiful fort that bears witness to tales of courage, valor, and sacrifice of its royalties and commoners. Jaisalmer is no exception; this was my second trip to the magnificent city, but I knew its 800-year-old fort would still bedazzle me with its exquisite beauty and grandeur.

This particular photograph, titled "Jaisalmer Fort Overlooking City," was taken atop one of the palace balconies. The late afternoon sun with the panoramic view overlooking the city of Jaisalmer and the Thar desert in the horizon and infinity, I knew I had to encapsulate this vision with a photograph that I could cherish forever, a photograph that would take me immediately to that palace balcony and provide the same intense euphoria that I had experienced.

–Rajat Kapoor

VICTORINE by Drēma Drudge

Now Available from Fleur-de-Lis Press

In 1863, Civil War is raging in the United States. Victorine Meurent is posing nude, in Paris, for paintings that will be heralded as the beginning of modern art: *Manet's Olympia* and *Picnic on the Grass*. However, Victorine's persistent desire is not to be a model but to be painter herself. In order to live authenically, she finds the strength to flout the expectations of her parents, bourgeios society and the dominant male artistist (whom she knows personally) while never losing her capacity for affection, kindness, and loyalty.

" . . . you will see a relationship between painter and model unfold with remarkable clarity and sensitivity."
—ELEANOR MORSE, author of *White Dog Fell from the Sky*

"Applying bold strokes of language, Drudge animates the story of a life lived at high intensity."
—JULIE BRICKMAN, author of *Two Deserts* and *What Only Birds Can Whisper*

Victorine is available from Fleur-de-Lis Press: www.louisvillereview.org. And in stores including Carmichael's Bookstores in Louisville, Kentucky, as well as Amazon and Barnes & Noble websites.